Treason Flight

T.R. Matson

~ For Isaac ~

No matter how tall the mountain, keep climbing.

Love, Dad

PREFACE

THIS IS A TALE OF LEADERSHIP.

Treason Flight follows a young navy pilot along the journey of a combat deployment. Along the way, he deals with members of his chain of command who put their self-interests ahead of the bigger picture and greater good of those they command. Life aboard a US Navy Aircraft Carrier, far away from the comforts of home, can only be truly appreciated by those who have experienced it. The stress, loneliness, and lack of privacy are offset by the comradery and closeness that brings with it lifelong friends. This comradery and common goal are the only things that get you through the day-to-day grind that is a combat deployment at sea.

During my decades of military service, I have held the highest levels of security clearances, and because of this I am required to submit anything I write that I intend for public release, including works of fiction, to the Department of Defense. This manuscript was submitted to the DOD Office of Prepublication and Security Review and was "cleared as amended." My intent with writing Treason Flight was to allow you, the reader, to follow along in a world that very few will experience firsthand. My intent was to never allow the enemy any advantage, tactical or otherwise, in the future that would put our servicemen and women in harm's way. I have taken great personal pride in ensuring that above all this was the case.

I am not Jack "Rattler" Owen, but many others and I that have walked in his shoes. I know his feelings and the absolute highs and lows that come with doing the job he was tasked with. While certain squadrons, ships and other US Navy institutions are mentioned, Treason

Flight's story is one of fiction as are the characters mentioned within. Any resemblance to actual people, living or dead, or actual events, is purely coincidental. Thank you for coming on this journey with me, and I hope you enjoy the story of a young man trying to serve his country with dignity and honor even when those who are tasked with leading him do not.

— T.R. Matson

Prologue

"602, you are at ten miles. Say needles," said the controller from the supercarrier USS *Nimitz.*

"602 negative needles," replied "Sickboy" from the right seat of the E-2C Hawkeye.

"602, fly bull's-eye," the controller replied.

"602," answered Sickboy. Given his inexperience, he knew this was not going to be an easy approach.

"Shit," mumbled "Rattler" from the left seat of the Hawkeye. He was already working hard to manage the aircraft, and this wasn't going to make it any easier.

"Huh?" questioned Sickboy.

"Nothing…" Rattler replied, wondering how bad his luck had to be to get him here. Maybe that was it—maybe his luck had run out. Throughout his career in the US Navy, he'd heard guys senior to him talk about a bucket of luck and a bucket of skill. You hoped the bucket of skill filled before the bucket of luck emptied. He used to laugh it off, but tonight, over the Persian Gulf in a broken E-2C Hawkeye with a very junior copilot and bad weather, he was starting to rethink the theory. Of course, now wasn't the time to think about this; he would have time for that later…hopefully.

"602, Paddles—you up?" radioed the landing signals officer (LSO) from the flight deck.

"Paddles, 602 has you loud and clear," replied Rattler, trying to place a name to the voice on the radio. It had to be "Grins." He was the senior LSO on the ship, and with tonight's conditions and this stupid Hawkeye giving him problems, he wouldn't want anyone else on the pickle to help him land.

"Hey, Rattler, it's Grins down here… When you get a chance, give me a rundown of what you are working, brother." Grins was a highly skilled Carrier Air Group (CAG) LSO, and Rattler really enjoyed working with him. The only downside to Grins in this circumstance was his background flying the F/A-18C Hornet. He had logged only one flight in the E-2C to see what the pilots were dealing with when they landed aboard the ship. That was the thing about Grins: he was always there to help and always trying to learn more. Most fighter pilots tended to be too busy or not interested enough to learn about the other aircraft being flown around every day; Grins was the opposite. He was also humble, and that's why he had "Clipper" out there with him on the LSO platform.

Clipper was Rattler's number two guy. They had gone to flight school together and ended up in the same fleet squadron. Rattler had arrived about six months sooner, and when Clipper got there, he started telling anyone who would listen that Clipper would be a great LSO. That's the thing about LSOs—it's kind of a fraternity in a squadron. There can only be a few at any given time, and most new guys or FNGs want to be one. Clipper was a natural fit. He was smart as hell (even though he was better at playing dumb), and honestly, if there was anyone in the squadron Rattler wanted on the platform right now, it was him. Rattler knew that Clipper was standing right next to Grins, listening and ready to give advice to help land the stricken Hawkeye.

"Paddles from 602, this is what's going on… Lost a hydraulic system at altitude, but honestly, man, I thought the gauge had frozen." (This had happened to Rattler numerous times, was a known issue, and really wasn't a big deal since there was still hydraulic fluid in the system. As the aircraft descended into warmer air, the gauge would unfreeze and start working again.) "But as we came down from altitude, nothing changed. At that time, the plane was flying fine and we started talking to the ship to get aboard ASAP. I worked on getting the aircraft configured. About fifteen miles behind the ship, I put the gear and flaps down. As soon as I heard the gear come down, the plane rolled into a sixty-degree angle of bank to the right. Took two hands and all my strength to get her level," Rattler explained.

"What the fuck did he just say?" yelled Clipper to Grins over the aircraft noise on the flight deck and the rescue helicopter starting up.

"602, Paddles, confirm your last…an uncommanded sixty-degree bank to the right?" Grins asked.

"Affirm, Paddles. We've got it configured now, but I'm having a hard time turning to the left. Something is either wrong with the hydraulics, flight controls, or something else, but she is being a real beast to keep straight," Rattler explained.

"All right buddy, how do you want to handle this?" Grins calmly asked over the radio, doing his best to hide his concern. Everyone on the ship was listening to this conversation, and Grins knew it was only a matter of time before he got a call from the Commander of the Carrier Air Group ("CAG" for short)—or worse, the skipper—giving their two cents about what to do. CAG was an old-school fighter pilot and could do amazing things with an aircraft. There wasn't much that CAG hadn't done or seen, but he had never been an LSO. While he could give advice, Grins was ultimately in control.

"Grins, I'd like to give it a shot. I plan on lining up left as I approach the ship and making small corrections to the right until I land. I know I'm working with a small window here, but if it looks bad, wave me off and I'll fly upwind and let the crew bail out, and then I'll ditch ahead of the ship." Rattler was matter-of-fact.

The E-2C Hawkeye's wingspan was eighty feet, while the width of the carrier's landing area was eighty-five feet. That would give Rattler 2 1/2 feet off of centerline before he risked hitting other aircraft, equipment, or the carrier tower. Grins knew that all nonessential personnel had already been ordered off, but he also knew that there were more lives at stake than just those aboard the Hawkeye. Grins looked over at Clipper. "Do you have any other ideas?"

"No—not unless they just bailout. Landing is risky for sure, but if anyone can do it, it's Rattler," shouted Clipper.

"602, copy all," radioed Grins. "We have a clear deck here and are ready for you. Listen to all LSO calls, and we will talk you down. Confirm you are configured gear down, full flaps for landing?"

"602, three down and locked; flaps full," replied Rattler. *Well, here goes nothing,* he thought.

Approaching six miles, Rattler now had a little time to brief the crew. As aircraft commander, everyone's safety was his responsibility. He was also the most senior member of the crew, not that he would need to assert that fact: everyone loved flying with Rattler. He had an ability to handle anything the E-2C could throw at him, keep his head, and take into account everyone's input before making a decision. He was the leader of the Junior Officer's Protection Association (JOPA), which was basically all of the junior officers in the squadron, and they looked up to him in one way or another. Now it was time for him to reassure them that everything would be OK...and maybe convince himself in the process.

"OK, let's get everyone up on the internal communication system (ICS)," said Rattler. "Here's how it's going to go. I'm going to do all the talking on the radio. Sickboy, I need you to watch that gauge. I don't care what happens—I need to know if our other system is starting to act funny. Everyone else, I'd really appreciate it if you were quiet, but if there's something you think I need to know, then tell me; let's not keep secrets here. I'm guessing that I will get one shot at this. The weather isn't great, but I should break out of the clouds about a mile or so behind the boat, and then I can work the lineup issues. If they wave me off, I bet they'll tell me to go upwind and level off and have you guys bail out. This would be a good time to mentally review your bailout procedures. I'll stick with the plane and ditch it ahead of the ship for the helicopter to come get me."

"I WILL STAY WITH YOU!" Sickboy exclaimed frantically.

"Sorry, buddy, but the navy has spent way too much on you for me to risk killing you in a ditch. You just got your three-year orders, and they'll be pissed if they have to find someone else to fill them," Rattler said with just a slight smile to break the sombre mood. "Plus, I need you to get in line at midnight rations (MIDRATS) because I'm going to need one of those famous sliders with an egg after this is all over. OK… So, anyone have any questions?"

The ensuing silence was Rattler's answer. He laughed to himself—after all, he had told them to try and keep quiet—but naval flight officers (NFOs) sure were a different breed. Since it was their job to radio ahead to the ship and get all of the logistics in place, he was really counting on them tonight.

"All right, buddy, let's go through that landing checklist one more time, because it would look stupid if I flew a perfect pass and forgot to put the hook down," Rattler said to Sickboy.

"Landing gear?"

"Three down and locked."

"Flaps?"

"Full."

"Hook?"

"Down."

"Landing checks complete," Sickboy affirmed.

"All right…no need to delay this any longer. Old Salt, 602 is four miles out and ready to come aboard," Rattler radioed.

"602, Paddles. Turn your taxi light on. We're currently going through a rainstorm," Grins advised.

"602," Rattler acknowledged. As Sickboy reached up for the switch, Rattler could only laugh once again. At a time like this, he would have thought that every fiber in his body would be tense, with nervousness or outright fear gripping his mind; in reality, he was finding humor in the dumbest things. With the whole Persian Gulf around, why wouldn't the skipper find an area where it wasn't raining? As if the low-lying cloud wasn't bad enough, the oil platforms and their burning fires gave the sense that he was flying upside down. *Let's just make this a little tougher.*

"Paddles, pick up!" screamed the commanding officer of the ship over the 5MC.

"Are you shitting me? Right now we have a lot going on!" said Clipper to no one in particular. That was the thing that Rattler liked about Clipper: he was a common-sense kind of person. Sure, he knew how to have fun—lots of it, actually—but when the shit hit the fan, Clipper was the sort of no-nonsense guy you wanted on your side.

Grins hung up the phone, reading Clipper's mind. "Skipper just wanted to know if we wanted him to go around and try again because of the rain."

"Doesn't he realize that this is serious shit? It's not like Rattler can just eject. They lose that other hydraulic system and the only thing the fighter pukes are going to be doing for the next few days is planning the missing-man formation flyby for the funerals," Clipper pointed out as he slammed his hand down against the control panel. He had a habit of doing that to clear his head and get back in the game…and it worked. He was back just in time to see the taxi light from 602 slowly breaking out of the clouds.

"602, Paddles: contact call the ball," radioed Clipper.

"602, Clara ship," replied Rattler, letting Clipper know that not only did he not have the Fresnel Lens in sight, but that he also couldn't see the ship yet—not an ideal situation when you're trying to land on it.

"602, you're on glide slope, lined up left."

Here is where it happens, thought Rattler as he began to make out the ship. "Ball!" he replied, but he knew that Clipper would talk him down the whole way anyway. *OK, small correction to the right, but nice and easy.*

"You're on glide slope, right for lineup."

OK that was the call…he was getting close, and it was time to get in the window. If he didn't make the correction right now, he'd risk hitting equipment or people on the left side of the landing area. Time slowed and then stopped. Rapid eye movement ensured that Rattler's gaze didn't stagnate. Keeping your eyes moving and noticing the corrections you need to make: that was the secret to good ball flying—otherwise, things could go bad…real quick.

“Here comes centerline,” radioed Clipper.

Time had slowed just enough for Rattler to think that Clipper had made a great call, and he was really proud of how good of an LSO he was becoming. But that thought was short-lived. As soon as Rattler put in the control input to stop his left-to-right drift, he realized the controls had stopped working. He had full aileron into the left wing, and the plane was still going right!

“Back to the left! COME LEFT! WAVE OFF! WAVE-OFF!!!” screamed Clipper, but it was too late. The drift was picking up speed, and Rattler and the stricken E-2C were only about a foot off the flight deck. His scan stopped as he saw the aircraft in front of him and then the tower. In a last-ditch effort, he slammed the left rudder pedal to the floor, and with it came his final thought: *God, please just take me.*

Chapter 1

Jack "Rattler" Owen grew up in a small suburban town in New Jersey with one older sister and a mother and father who ran their own business. They taught him early on that hard work and never giving up was all you needed to be successful. Although he was raised in a small automotive shop learning how to change oil and pump gas, he had dreams of something bigger. He didn't want to ever work for a living; he wanted to get paid to have fun, and his plan revolved around football.

Blessed with a linebacker's frame, he enjoyed success early on, and it drove everything he did. All the time spent in the gym and studying game plays were all for one thing: to make it to the NFL. Could he have been a superstar if he'd been blessed with more natural ability? Sure, but what Rattler lacked in natural talent he made up for in hard work. In fact, throughout his life, it was the example set by his parents and sister that kept him focused. Yet, underneath all of the success was the fear of not living up to their expectations. The only way he could overcome that was to work even harder.

Rattler was no genius, but things came pretty easy for him. He remembered many times when his sister Melissa would get angry because of how little he studied only to get the same grades as she did. Rattler just shrugged it off because he was focused on other things. He had hopes of going to the high school down the street from his house, the same high school that his mother had attended. But at the last minute, he was told, "Catholic school or military school." Looking back now at what the Catholic schoolgirls wore, he likes to say that he made the wrong choice, but the thought of being disciplined by the nuns drove him to pick military school. His sister had gone to the same school and had graduated as valedictorian, so how hard could it be? However, the next four years would prove to be the wakeup call that Rattler needed.

Rattler's sister had been the first student to transfer into this particular military school without starting as a freshman. They'd told her to expect her straight As to drop to Cs and Ds. Well, if there was anything you wanted Melissa to do, just tell her that she couldn't do it and stand back. Two years later, she graduated at the top of her class *and* kept all her straight As. Five years after that, enter Rattler. When the school saw the last name "Owen," they expected the same performance they'd seen from Melissa. Well, that was not going to be the case. Being yelled at and pushing yourself on the football field was one thing because it made sense to Rattler, but when it came to some upperclassman yelling at him because his shoes were too wet (it was raining at the time), he couldn't wrap his mind around it.

Shortly after arriving, he began to buck the system, and although he did graduate four years later, he was much closer to the bottom of his class than the top. He made one vow right before he walked across the stage to get his diploma: "I WILL NEVER JOIN THE MILITARY!" and with that, he was off to a small school in eastern Pennsylvania—partially because his football dreams were now over and partly because he'd become more interested in women than anything else.

After an abysmal first year at college in eastern Pennsylvania, Rattler realized that he needed to get things on track or he would end up with no future prospects. His focus shifted back to the military. He vaguely remembered all the flying stories he'd heard from his high school instructors and thought that maybe he could do that. He was reasonably fit and could get back into football shape quickly. School had never really challenged him, so how hard could the math of flying be? And he had good eyesight, so why not? Before he knew it, he was far away from home, arriving for his first day at Texas A&M.

"HOWDY!" yelled the woman across the grass field.

"Hi," Rattler replied. He would soon learn that "howdy" was a common Texas A&M greeting, but this was going to take some getting used to because where he grew up, you didn't talk to others; you just kept to yourself and went about your business. In the South, everyone was friendly, and he began to like it. Looking back, college was a blur of Navy ROTC and drinking. He still wanted to have a good time, but he was focused on getting his pilot slot in the navy and not letting anything or anyone get in the way.

Keeping his distance from most women seemed to work until he met Jennifer Phillips. Their relationship was a typical one for a college couple. Although he graduated two years before her, she would eventually meet him in south Texas, and they would marry and start moving around the country together. It didn't surprise anyone that she followed him while he finished flight school and began training on the E-2C Hawkeye in Norfolk, Virginia. Ultimately, they ended up at Point Mugu, California, where Rattler was assigned to the Wallbangers of VAW-117. Of course, all of that seemed so long ago…

CHAPTER 2

"You can come back on the power, 602. We've got you," radioed the air boss from his bird's-eye view of the flight deck.

Rattler's eyes slowly opened to see a familiar scene in front of him—a yellow shirt frantically trying to get him to come back on the power so they could push him back and disconnect the arresting hook from the cable. He couldn't believe it. Was this some sort of dream? Surely heaven can't be an aircraft carrier flight deck…at night.

Crap, those nuns in Catholic church were right… This is hell, Rattler thought as Sickboy's voice penetrated his dazed mind.

"You OK, man? I think they want us out of the landing area."

"Yeah, I'm fine—sorry. You're clear on the flaps and wings," Rattler replied.

Sickboy went about his copilot duties, stowing the flaps and folding the wings as Rattler carefully taxied the plane out of the landing area and forward onto catapult two to shut down. Once the plane was chained to the flight deck, the engines were shut down and everyone got out to begin their normal post-flight tasks. Rattler spoke with the plane captain and flight deck chief to explain the problems he'd encountered with his aircraft, but mid-sentence, AMC Davis interrupted him. "Sorry, sir, we will not sleep tonight until we figure out what happened up there. We're just lucky that you were at the controls. It won't happen again, I promise you that!"

"It's OK, Chief. Just let me know if I can help at all with the troubleshooting, and don't keep the boys up too late trying to figure it out. We have other planes we can fly." Rattler smiled as he walked toward the edge of the flight deck, on his way down to the ready room. He knew that no matter what he said, those young kids would be up all night trying to fix that plane.

As he entered ready room two, Clipper caught Rattler's eye: one look and Clipper knew this was as serious as he'd suspected.

"Nice job, bro." Clipper broke the momentary silence.

"Thanks for being there, Paddles. Couldn't have done it without you," Rattler replied.

"We already have a slider, and a nice bottle of relaxation ready to be opened in the room when you get down there," Clipper hinted.

It is against the rules to have alcohol on a navy ship, unless of course it's part of the ship's stash used for parties, and for sucking up to high-powered VIPs while in foreign ports. So, to say that Rattler and Clipper and the rest of their six-man room of junior officers were going to break open a bottle of vodka and relive what Rattler had just experienced all over again would be wrong. So, they didn't do that. They drank water, or maybe bug juice, had their food, and tried to figure out what could have caused that problem in the plane. The youngest of the group, "Rat-breath," had a way of saying what everyone was thinking.

"Fuck, man… I can't get over how you guys could have died. I mean, you aren't normally going to recover a plane with control problems like that; all five of you would have been swimming, or dead."

Complete silence filled the room. After what seemed like minutes, but was in reality only seconds, Clipper broke the tension. "Yeah, but it was Rattler flying. Nothing's going to get him. He's invincible."

"Yeah, yeah…yeah, I am," replied Rattler, after which he stood up and went to bed. This day needed to be over. There was just too much shit going on right now for him to deal with. After crawling into his rack and putting on his headphones, he lay there staring at the ceiling and thinking about why he'd made it. *I guess I just take a little more luck out of the bucket.*

Rattler couldn't have been asleep long before he woke up to the ringing of the phone in his stateroom. Much like every time it rings, he figured everyone in the room would pretend to be asleep and hope that someone else would get it. To his surprise, the call was answered quickly. He could hear Clipper's side of the conversation.

"Yeah, he's not feeling too well. OK, sure. Yeah, I will help instead. Nope, I'll be up there in a minute. Nope, he doesn't need the flight doc." There was silence and then the phone was hung up. Clipper moved around in the darkness, trying to get his flight suit on. Rattler peeked out from behind the curtain.

"What's up, dude?" Rattler asked.

"Nothing, man. Maintenance wanted you to come up to the flight deck and turn the aircraft and try to replicate what happened tonight. No way I'm having you up there after all that calming bug juice, so I'll do it. Get some sleep, bro."

"Thanks, man. I owe you one." And with that, Rattler fell back to sleep.

CHAPTER 3

BANG!!!

"Fuck, ugh," Rattler said aloud as he woke to what sounded like the first catapult shots of the day. Even down here on the O-2 level, it was pretty loud. He always thought of the new guys living on the O-3 level right under the flight deck—poor bastards. He climbed out of his rack and went about washing his face, trying to wake up.

"Fucking Clipper's bug juice," he mumbled. He put on his flip flops and grabbed his towel, shower bag, and room key, and made his way out to the bathroom to try to get in a shower before seeing what was on the schedule for today. As soon as he got to the bathroom, he saw that it was going to be another "Fine Navy Day" as he read the "Closed for Cleaning" sign on the door. He made his way back to his room and did a navy bath at the sink before putting on his flight suit and boots. Subconsciously, he checked to make sure his dog tags and cross were in his pocket.

His Aunt Ellie had given him that cross after he got his Wings of Gold in Kingsville, Texas, telling him that it was blessed by a local priest. She asked him if he would always carry it when he went flying. From that day on, the cross was in his flight-suit pocket whenever he left the ground—pilots can be superstitious that way. Heck, Rattler had friends who were so superstitious, they would go out of their way *not* to be superstitious. Of course, the flip side was also true. A good friend in flight school had told him not to wash the luck out of his flight suits. At first, Rattler hadn't believed him, but ultimately, once they'd moved in together and summertime had come to south Texas, he understood that his friend wasn't kidding.

Rattler hadn't even made it into ready room two, home of the Wallbangers while on the USS *Nimitz*, before Clipper grabbed him.

"Dude, Skipper is pissed and 'Shotgun' is going to CAG. We need to talk so you are filled in." He grabbed Rattler's arm, steering him away from the ready room and into the forward wardroom where they'd have some privacy.

"So here's the deal…" Clipper began.

"Bro, give me a second to get a cup of coffee and try to clear my head. I have to wave today, and it sounds like they have already launched planes," Rattler replied.

"Dude, man, I've got you covered. You can wave if you want, but the whole ship is talking about last night, and they are saying some shit about you and how you handled it. Grins is not expecting you on the LSO platform until the second recovery. We sent Ratbreath up there to get some training in your place. First things first. Get your coffee, and I have to tell you what happened in the ready room this morning," Clipper insisted.

With that, Rattler made his way over to the giant coffee maker and poured a large cup. Rattler didn't take the small things in life for granted, and he smiled about how he'd never liked coffee until he deployed. Now, he drank that shit like water in order to stay focused and awake. Oh, the joys of navy life. He searched around the wardroom for something to eat and ended up with two apples, since breakfast was over and lunch was not scheduled to be served for another hour.

He made his way back to where Clipper was sitting and could feel the energy coming off his friend. Rattler had known Clipper long enough to realize that when he was this excited, one of two things had happened: either Clipper had just gotten laid, or there'd been an incident involving the higher-ranking officers that made them look even more like the piss-poor leaders they were. Mental preparations over, Rattler sat down.

"Go ahead, but talk slowly. I'm still waking up."

"All right, bud. So, this morning I get up early, because honestly, I couldn't sleep last night. I went up to check out the airplane, and that hydraulic system was shit, dude. The thing literally came apart when I started up the plane and put the system under some load. AMC Davis was sitting right next to me when the thing popped and started pissing hydraulic fluid everywhere. You were lucky man…real lucky."

"OK, cool. So you drag me in here to tell me that my chances of dying last night were higher than I thought. Thanks, bro, but I have things to do," Rattler explained as he pushed his chair back to stand up.

"Dude, man, you know me better than that. Sit down bro dingo, and let me get to the good part. So I went into maintenance control this morning to see if they had learned anything more as to why the part failed, and I see Skipper coming out of his stateroom with Shotgun from the maintenance department. *No big deal really*, is what I think first. I figure maybe they are on the same mission planning team or something, right? But then, right after they pass maintenance control, I hear Shotgun say to Skipper: 'With all due respect, sir, you knew this was going to happen when that maintenance report was put on your desk; you chose to ignore the underlying problem with your squadron. I think Rattler deserves the award, and the fact that you won't put him in for it because you don't have one yourself is complete bullshit.' Then, Skipper turns around and tells him to mind his own business. Of course, at this point I am intrigued, so after Skipper leaves, I go find Shotgun to see what's up. Between us, bro, he told Skipper you deserve a flying cross for that shit you did last night. And our chicken-shit skipper said he wouldn't put you in for one because he has never gotten one himself. Can you believe that shit, man? It's unreal…" Clipper trailed off.

"Clipper, man, YN1 has a question for you." Sickboy appeared at the door of the wardroom.

"All right, man. I'll be there in a second," Clipper replied. As Clipper turned back, he saw that Rattler hadn't moved from the table. He was still trying to digest what he'd been told. "You OK, man?"

"Yeah, dude. I'll be fine. Gonna finish up my coffee and head to the platform to get some fresh air. Thanks for the info. I'll catch up with you later," Rattler assured him.

"Dubai in a couple more days, man. We've got to teach these new guys how to party," Clipper said, doing his best to lighten the mood.

Rattler smiled back. "For sure."

And with that, Clipper was gone, moving with his predictable, enviable energy. The only exception to that was after he'd eaten a ton of ice cream in the wardroom. Clipper was lactose intolerant, but he also loved ice cream. No matter how much the rest of the stateroom would complain, he would eat ice cream and enjoy every mouthful. His roommates would pay the price later.

As Rattler sat there, finishing his coffee, he couldn't help but wonder two things. First, could the story of Shotgun and Skipper be 100 percent true? And second, which maintenance report was Shotgun talking about? Rattler had certainly not heard about anything, and he worked in the maintenance department. Sure, it was a tough landing, but there were other pilots who could have handled it; Rattler didn't view his skills as extraordinary. He would regularly refer to himself as a "blue collar pilot," meaning that he'd worked as hard as anyone else to achieve success.

Even if the aircraft was in that much distress and people thought he deserved something for his actions, did his skipper really say no because of jealousy? There was no way that Skipper could be that bad. They'd had their run-ins, but he always believed Skipper would do the right thing when push came to shove. As Rattler sat there drinking coffee that could be used to power an aircraft, he couldn't help but remember a particular situation in an Alaskan detachment many months before. The skipper had been fairly new to the squadron and had tried to impress everyone with his tactical knowledge. Being a nerd is one thing, but covering up maintenance problems and not duly recognizing members of his squadron was something else entirely.

Chapter 4

"Damn, I thought it was summertime!" Rattler said to no one in particular as he walked out to the E-2C sitting on the tarmac, ready for the early flight. They had been in Elmendorf, Alaska, for only a few days, and this would be his first flight here. He was looking forward to taking in the much-talked-about views, or at the very least, seeing what he could since the weather was complete crap. For some reason, the clouds looked more ominous than they ever did in California.

This was supposed to be the first large force exercise of the detachment, including Navy F/A-18 Hornets, as well as Air Force F-15, F-16, and F-22 aircraft. For this day's mission, the guys in the back of Rattler's aircraft would control the Navy F/A-18s as they went up against the Air Force F-22s. This was the first exercise that the F-22 Raptor was participating in; Rattler figured it would be a bloodbath since the radar and weapons of the Raptor were superior to that of the Super Hornet. Of course, the Raptor couldn't land on an aircraft carrier, so Rattler had no use for it.

Once he'd decided that military aviation was for him, Rattler had immediately turned to the navy. There was a certain appeal to being able to take off and land on an aircraft carrier. Sure, the perks of the air force might be better golf courses and colder beer, but he was out for adventure. After finishing primary flight training at Vance AFB in Enid, Oklahoma (as a joint venture training course), Rattler wanted to fly jets. His second choice was the E-2C because he wanted to travel the world and take off and land on the ship at night. Little did he know how challenging that would be.

As he approached the tarmac this particular morning, he noticed that the aircraft commander, LT Nicole "Revlon" Poole, was already out at the plane. She seemed ready to get the exercise over with. Rattler liked flying with Revlon because she was a good pilot and also very down-to-earth.

"Hey, Nicole, you ready for this?" Rattler asked.

"Ugh, I don't know. I got into a heated discussion with the skipper, which is why I am out here early—just didn't want to be around him. Did you know that most of the other aircraft are canceling due to the weather? The Raptors aren't going up in this," she replied.

"WHAT?! Then who are we 'fighting,' and why are we putting ourselves through this? I know I am still the FNG, but doesn't this weather seem a little too much if there is no real mission?" Rattler saw Revlon looking over his shoulder. He turned just in time to see their skipper walking up, and luckily, just in time to shut his mouth before he said something he would regret.

"Morning, Skipper," they said together.

"The plane is ready to go, but I'm a little concerned about the ice on the wings," Revlon said.

"That's not my concern. That's your job as stick monkeys. Deal with it." The skipper walked toward the Hawkeye's entry door, disappearing into the black hole that was the back part of the plane.

"All this daylight was probably getting to him. Sometimes, I think he is like a vampire," Rattler joked. Revlon returned a smile before she got onboard the plane to continue her pre-flight checks.

Rattler surveyed the sky again, aware of a bad feeling in his gut. *Maybe I'll just do an extra careful pre-flight,* he thought.

After spending what seemed like forever outside, Rattler confirmed that the plane was ready; of course it was. He was in charge of the line division at VAW-117, and he had the best young men and women working for him. As he climbed aboard the E-2C, he felt inside his left flight-suit pocket to make sure his lucky cross was in there. It was. The start-up, taxi, and takeoff were all uneventful. Soon, Rattler found himself lost in the duties of an E-2C pilot while sitting on mission profile.

"I'm showing us 1,000 pounds above our planned fuel," Revlon mentioned.

"Roger. Just another boring flight, huh?" Rattler replied.

"I hope so, but these clouds aren't looking like they are going to break up at all. I'm going to call weather and get an update; try to listen to the guys in the back and see if they are actually controlling anything," Revlon said.

While Revlon conferred with the controller about weather over Alaska, Rattler went about searching the numerous radios to find the frequency that the NFOs were using. After a little search, he gave up and called his buddy, Eric "Spike" Morris in the back of the plane to find out. Spike had been in the squadron about as long as Rattler and was given his call sign because every time they would go out drinking, he would fetch anything—more beer, cigarettes, women, whatever—Spike would deliver. He was a good dog.

"Hey, bro, what radio are you guys working?" Rattler asked Spike.

"Ha! Working? Not really, man. There are two Super Hornets up here and that's it. Both have no working radar so they are completely 'lead nose,' and the skipper is just having them fly around to see if the weather is any better anywhere. He won't even let me have my scope on a scale where I can see them. Such a waste, man. Do you have anything to do after we land? I am going to need some beers to make up for hanging out with the mad man for five hours," Spike replied.

"Geez, seriously? Unreal, man. What a waste. We are in freaking Alaska, and we are wasting our time up here. Anyway, I have no plans after landing, so let's grab some food and more beers to make this day go away. And do me a favor; keep an eye on the mad man back there. My guess is that his head is so far up his own ass right now that he wouldn't recognize if those Super Hornets joined up and flew formation on us," Rattler continued.

"No problem, man. It's almost beer thirty; talk to you soon." Spike signed off.

As Rattler directed his attention back to Revlon, he could see that she was finishing up her radio conversation too. She was a good-looking woman and that was saying something, coming from Rattler. He was definitely a fan of the opposite sex, but there were two things about Rattler that no one would deny. First, he had no interest in any woman in uniform. You could take the most beautiful woman in the world and put her in a uniform, and he just lost interest. Maybe it was the practical side of him realizing how hard a relationship would be with someone in the military, or maybe just too many days at military school. Second, he had an undying love for his wife, Jennifer. From the moment he laid his eyes on her at Texas A&M University, he was hooked. In a stroke of luck, his friend met her roommate and that gave him the "in" that he needed. That's what made these detachments so tough: he'd just gotten home from his first deployment after finishing training and becoming fully qualified in the Hawkeye, and now he was up here for a month in the cold of Alaska, away from the woman he loved. Oh well, he would be home soon.

"Weather is getting worse and quick. We need to head back," Revlon said with urgency.

"OK, I talked with Spike, and they aren't controlling anyone. The two Super Hornets are just looking for clear air and are lead nose, so I vote we head home," Rattler replied.

"OK, I'll tell Skipper," Revlon said as she took a deep breath, knowing this was not going to go well.

Revlon called Skipper on the ICS. "CICO Flight…"

"STAND BY!" Skipper replied.

"Probably a sale on pocket protectors or something else extremely nerdy back there," Rattler said to Revlon, which finally made her laugh.

"Go ahead, but make it quick," Skipper called back.

"Sir, I am showing most of the strike package was a weather abort, and I just talked to metro and the weather is getting worse, so we are going to head home. I am taking a westerly course now back to base," Revlon said.

"Stand by!" Skipper fired back, and he was gone.

"So, do you think he means stand by on going home, or stand by to talk more?" Revlon asked.

"I don't care. I really don't like how these clouds look, and I have a bad feeling about this. My vote is home," Rattler replied. He looked over in the right seat and could tell that Revlon was not enjoying making this decision. He wondered how he would handle it when he was an aircraft commander. Luckily, he didn't have to worry about that today. He continued to look at Revlon to see what she was going to do and couldn't help but think that his eyes were playing tricks on him. He'd had very little sleep the previous night so he was tired, but he hadn't gone out drinking or anything. It was just that the sun was basically up all day and night, and he hadn't been able to buy anything to black out the windows in his room yet. But there was something out there off the right side of the aircraft, and as he strained his eyes to see past Revlon who was working the radios, hoping Skipper would call her back, his brain started to make sense of what he was seeing. *No, it can't be… I mean, we are alone in our piece of sky per the mission planning. But it kind of looks like—*

"SHIT!" Rattler said as he slammed the control yoke full forward, causing the Hawkeye to buck and moan and then kick off autopilot, giving the whole crew the feeling of weightlessness. Just as Revlon reacted and started to speak, a flight of two Super Hornets passed directly overhead the Hawkeye. With the jets rocketing by only fifty feet or so above them, a catastrophic midair collision was narrowly avoided. Rattler fought to keep the Hawkeye in control as he leveled off and then immediately scanned the sky to find the Super Hornets again. There were only two other aircraft in this whole military operating area, and they'd almost hit them. *How is that possible?* The Hornet had a better airborne radar system than most other planes… Of course, they were lead nose and Skipper was controlling them.

"OK, we are heading home," was the first thing Revlon could get out of her mouth. Just then, Skipper interrupted.

"Flight, CICO!" Skipper yelled.

"Yes, sir," Revlon replied.

"What are you damn stick monkeys doing up there? You are messing up my radar picture," Skipper continued.

"Sir, a flight of two Super Hornets almost hit us. They came out of nowhere. Do you have them on radar?" she asked.

"Stand by!" and with that, Skipper was gone again.

Rattler had already turned the plane to the west and was heading back to base. During the transit back, Rattler and Revlon kept the conversation to a minimum. When faced with a similar experience, no doubt most aviators tended to reflect almost immediately. Rattler and Revlon were doing just that, but they also had their hands full getting the plane back on the ground.

At 23,000 feet, they'd immediately noticed ice forming on the wings. Revlon worked diligently to try and keep the ice from accumulating while Rattler flew the aircraft. Wind shear began around 15,000 feet, which caused the aircraft to yaw violently from side to side, and to make matters worse, weather reports from the base had the winds just at the crosswind limit for the Hawkeye. After what seemed like forever, Rattler felt the wheels slam into the runway. The aircraft slowly came under control, and its speed decreased. He exhaled for what felt like the first time in at least thirty minutes.

The taxi back to the hangar was uneventful and quick. Soon, the aircraft was shut down, and the crew was able to exit. Standing outside to meet them was the executive officer (XO) Commander Richard "Spool" Collins. It was rumored that he got the call sign "Spool" because of his overt calmness—nothing seemed to rattle him. As the skipper walked up to him, Rattler was just exiting the Hawkeye; he overheard their brief exchange.

"I want both of those pilots grounded until further notice!" Skipper said to XO as he walked by.

"Good flight?" Spool asked Revlon and Rattler as they approached. "Don't worry about him. He was probably worried about his radar picture, right? You know how NFOs can be. They are just a different breed. Is everyone OK?"

"Yes, sir," Revlon answered.

"OK, go and get out of your flight gear and see if you can skip the debrief. I've got some beer back at the rooms, and I'm having the squadron over…well, most of them anyway," XO said.

"Yes, sir!" both Rattler and Revlon said together as they began their long walk back to the gear shop.

"Hey, Rattler!" XO yelled.

"Sir?" Rattler replied.

"Nice landing, kid. I came out here because I knew you guys were coming back, and this weather is about as dog shit as you'll see up here. From my vantage point, you handled it like a pro. Keep it up, man."

"Yes, sir!" Rattler replied. He tried to hold back a smile as Revlon slapped him on the back.

"They're going to make you an LSO, you know that, right? You've got the flying skills, and I think you'd be good at it," Revlon declared. "Now, let's go and get something to drink and try to forget about what we just went through."

CHAPTER 5

"One hundred!" yelled Ratbreath, ensuring the controlling LSO knew the landing area was still not clear for the next aircraft. Rattler walked up the ladder to the flight deck and into the sunlight. He always loved being outside the skin of the ship. Many days would pass out here in the middle of the ocean, and Rattler always wondered how the ship's company could handle being on the "boat" without the freedom of going flying. *Impossible,* he thought. If he ever lost the ability to fly, he would be out of the navy as quickly as possible. He likened his situation to a prison sentence: at least he got to go out into the yard and work out. Flying was the highlight of his day, and he imagined, of every aviator's day, for that manner.

"One hundred!" yelled Ratbreath again. He was taking his training seriously and coming along nicely. Rattler smiled to himself as he thought of his pick for the next LSO, knowing that Ratbreath would be a good fit. There would be a little bit of a gap in new guys showing up at the squadron, so the next slot to fill would be that of an LSO. An E-2C squadron typically had four LSOs at one time, all engaged in different levels of training while guys rotated into and out of the squadron. Ratbreath had shown up at the same time as another pilot, so it had been up to Rattler to give his recommendation to the skipper. Rattler had chosen correctly.

As Rattler walked around the jet blast deflector and onto the LSO platform, he felt at home. The smell of jet exhaust, fuel, sweat, metal, and whatever else the Persian Gulf had to offer assaulted his nose all at once...and he loved every bit of it. He watched his LSO team working hard on the platform as an F/A-18C came around the approach turn and set up for landing. It was a beautiful day and extremely hot already. The seas were dead calm, and the winds seemed perfect. If he couldn't be flying today, at least he could be up here. He heard stories about guys who didn't even see the light of day for weeks while on deployment. That was not for him.

"Gear, lens set 360 Hornet, clear deck!" yelled the only enlisted man on the platform, all the rest being officers and LSOs. With that call, the young man confirmed that the arresting gear and lens were set for the correct aircraft and that the landing area was clear. This became routine, but was extremely critical for the landing to be successful. If the gear wasn't set properly, it could damage the aircraft or the arresting gear and send the aircrew into the ocean. If the lens wasn't set properly, the aircraft would be on the wrong glide path and risked being too high, or worse, hitting the back of the ship. Finally, the last step in the chain was ensuring the deck was clear.

There had been at least one horrible, nighttime mishap where one aircraft landed on another that was still in the landing area. All members of both crews had died, so a clear deck was everything to an LSO. As Ratbreath came back along the LSO platform, his job was to scan the landing area for the other LSOs to ensure the deck stayed clear. If anyone or anything went into the landing area, Ratbreath's vigilance was key to letting the other LSOs know. This time, as he came back to his post, Ratbreath was concentrating too much on the Hornet on final, which was easy to do. With all the action happening behind the ship, it took discipline to look the other way, but this step was critical. Rattler walked over to Ratbreath and tapped him on the shoulder.

"Keep looking forward, bro. I know it's boring, but you will save lives that way, trust me," Rattler said.

"Sorry, man," Ratbreath replied. He went back to his job of scanning forward and aft, as he should.

Within seconds, the Hornet came crashing down, putting his arresting hook right between the #2 and #3 wire for a perfect pass. *Man, it would be fun to fly that aircraft one day,* Rattler thought.

As the other LSOs went about recording the landing grade and critiquing the pilot (which all had to be done within about 45 seconds because the next aircraft was already coming around the approach turn), Rattler went up to Grins and stood next to him. Grins felt his presence. They hadn't spoken since Rattler's close-call landing the night before.

"Hey, buddy! How are you doing?" Grins said.

"I'm good, man. I don't need to control this recovery... Just needed some fresh air," Rattler explained.

"Yeah, I bet last night was some shit, huh?" Grins commented.

"Eh, just another day flying the mighty Hawkeye," Rattler replied.

"Gear, lens set 460 Rhino," yelled the enlisted man.

Both Grins and Rattler instinctually turned toward the back of the ship to make sure it actually was a Super Hornet or "Rhino" on final. It was.

"Clear deck, Rhino!" Ratbreath yelled and stepped toward the back of the LSO platform.

Rattler watched another perfect pass, marking the last plane in this recovery phase. It was most likely the CAG coming in; that guy sure could fly. As he landed, snagging the #3 wire, the other LSOs began to make their way off the platform. They now had to go below and walk the length of the ship, visiting each ready room and debriefing every pilot who had just landed. All the grades would need to be put into the computer before coming back up in less than an hour. This cycle would continue all day and night—such was the life of an LSO and not one of them would trade it for anything, except maybe an extra flight. Rattler took a step toward the flight deck in order to make his way downstairs, and Grins grabbed his arm.

"Hey man, I'm not kidding. That was some pretty amazing instincts you had last night. I've watched the video probably twenty-five times. You were headed straight for the ship's tower and somehow, you got it to land. Unreal. CAG was really impressed," Grins said.

"CAG was watching it with you?" Rattler said, shocked.

"Yeah, man. He was very interested in how you handled the plane with such a controllability problem. He brought in every E-2C pilot on his staff and started quizzing them on how the E-2C works and what could have gone wrong. Every one of them said that what you did was amazing," Grins replied.

"Well, thanks, man. I just did what made sense. I don't know what I was really thinking, but I thought we were done for," Rattler said as he looked down at the flight deck, reliving the horrible moments from the night before.

"Listen, man, you can wave as much or as little as you want up here today. I know this is your LSO team and your day to wave, but if you are not feeling it, take a break," Grins said after a moment.

"No way, man. What am I going to do? Sit in my room all day and scroll through Clipper's disturbingly large hard drive full of movies?" Rattler quipped.

"Ha! Well, that could kill some time for sure." Grins laughed.

"I'll be up here for the third recovery. I'm going to hit the gym and get out a little aggression on the weights, and then I'll be good to go. Can you handle it without me until then?" Rattler asked.

"Sure thing, man. Go get huge!" Grins answered.

Rattler turned to walk off the flight deck as Grins yelled, "Hey bro, don't be surprised if CAG wants to talk to you later about last night!"

"Roger," Rattler replied. He just wanted that flight behind him and the spotlight to be off, but that was unlikely unless something even crazier happened to someone else today. That was life at sea: you were the talk of the town until the next big event. Whenever a pilot missed all the wires, or boltered and had to make a second attempt at landing, that pilot couldn't wait until the next person did the same thing so that people would forget his mistake. Everything was news on the ship and word traveled fast, but there was always another headline right around the corner. That was how it was in the dynamic world at sea.

CHAPTER 6

"Our hero!" yelled a rather drunk Sickboy as Rattler walked into the admin, a large hotel suite that the squadron junior officers all chipped in for when the ship pulled into port. They had been out at sea for over sixty days, and everyone was ready for a little R&R.

"Thanks, man. Sounds like you new guys got the place set up nicely and got the party started early," Rattler replied humbly.

"No, seriously man—anything that you ever need, I'm here, man. I guess I didn't really see it at the time, but everyone has been talking about it since. You are the best damn Hawkeye pilot in the navy! I wrote an email to my wife and told her the whole story, and she told me to give you a hug," Sickboy rambled between swigs from his beer.

"How about just a beer, man?" Rattler said, hoping that this wasn't going to turn into a hugging session.

"Sure thing! I'll be right back!" and Sickboy was off. Rattler had to hand it to the new guys for finding this place. It wasn't just a hotel room but the penthouse suite at one of the biggest hotels in Dubai. Somehow, they'd managed to convince the owner that they were defending the free world and had been upgraded to this suite for their four-day port call. Not a bad move, even for new guys.

"Here you go, man," Sickboy said as he handed Rattler a beer. Just then, Clipper came in the front door with a girl on each arm.

"Rattler! Meet Sandy and Cheri. They are Australian flight attendants who are here on a layover and said they want to meet the American pilot who is making headlines all over the news," Clipper said with a smile.

"What? Seriously?!" Rattler said as he turned red and stood up.

"No, dude. Come on… You are good, but not that good. They just want to hang out and party with some Yankee pilots for the night." Clipper laughed.

"Hey man, can I talk to you?" Rattler asked.

"Sure, man. Hey ladies, go in the back room and get a drink. Sick-boy, take care of these girls and treat them good. They are the future Mrs. Clipper and Rattler," Clipper exclaimed. The girls giggled; Clipper grabbed Rattler's arm, and they walked out into the hallway.

Once outside, Clipper was all business. He was a man on a mission when it came to girls, and he had clearly laid down some pretty good roadwork. He didn't want it wasted by someone else in the admin getting the girls interested while he stood out here talking to Rattler.

"What's up, man?" Clipper asked.

"Hey, man—I appreciate what you are doing, but things are just a blur right now. I mean, I'm still dealing with that flight the other night and all the stuff going on at home…" Rattler trailed off. It had been almost four months since his wife, Jennifer, had filed for divorce, literally one week after he'd left for deployment. He didn't want to go home and deal with it, so his lawyer had fast-tracked all the paperwork, and they had two more months before it was final. Coming out of nowhere, it had hit him like a ton of bricks, and everyone in the squadron was surprised—everyone except for Clipper, that is. He never liked Jennifer. He'd never said anything to Rattler about it, but Rattler knew anyway. Clipper was definitely not about to let Jennifer ruin Rattler's chance to have some Australian guilt-free fun while in port.

"DUDE, no! I'm not listening to this, man. OK, I've kept this to myself for long enough, but we are bros and I'm telling you how I feel. She's a bitch, man. You literally did everything for her, and she treated you like shit. I know you are gone a lot, but she knew that before she married you. She signed up for this just like we did and she knew it would suck at times, but she quit on you, and she didn't even have the guts to tell you in person. She had to wait until we left and then send you an email! No way, dude. Now, Sandy in there has sixty hours here in Dubai before she flies back to Australia, and she is awesome. I mean tall, blonde, looks like a damn model for Christ's sake, and did you hear that accent? Did you?" Clipper fired off wildly.

Clipper continued as Rattler's thoughts wandered to his soon-to-be ex-wife. Clipper had a point: Rattler had been a great husband—as good as one can expect while being gone all the time. He bought her anything she wanted, and when he was home, he would do anything for her. Yet, since they moved out to California, she seemed distant. It was almost like she was turning into a flashy California girl. Even though Rattler didn't like it, he always let her do whatever she wanted, and where had that left him? With an empty house, an empty bank account, and an empty heart.

Rattler's parents had stayed together through thick and thin, running a successful business together. Although they'd had their fights, they always worked through it. By the time Jennifer sent that email, she was already done; she wasn't going to try to work through things no matter how much Rattler begged. The paperwork was filed and that was it. They were now two-thirds of the way through their California-mandated cooling off period, and there was nothing that was going to stop the divorce from going through. So, maybe getting to know Sandy wasn't such a bad idea.

"So, seriously, man, give me one good reason why you shouldn't get to know her?" Clipper pressed.

Rattler's mind finished wandering and came back to the conversation. "I don't have one, man. So, flight attendant, you say?" Rattler repeated with a smile.

"YES! Now, let's get back in there and have some fun!" Clipper slapped Rattler's back and opened the door. "It's good to have you back, bro…damn good."

As they entered the room, Clipper introduced Sandy and Cheri to Rattler again. After some small talk, Sandy lightly touched Rattler's arm and whispered into his ear, "How did you get your call sign?"

Rattler smiled and looked at her, and when their eyes met, he said, "Why don't we go somewhere quieter and I will tell you the story?" With that, they grabbed two more beers. Sandy took Rattler's hand and led him out of the admin. On their way out, Rattler caught Clipper's eye in one of those unique moments when two friends who were closer than brothers knew exactly what the other was thinking. *It is good to be back*, Rattler thought.

CHAPTER 7

It was amazing how many stars you could see, even in a city. Rattler looked upward, transfixed; he couldn't take his eyes away even though there was something (or someone) much more beautiful to look at right next to him. They had been up on the rooftop for about fifteen minutes.

"So, are you going to tell me the story of your call sign?" Sandy asked, breaking the silence and startling Rattler.

He was taken aback a little and immediately became embarrassed when he realized how lost in thoughts he had been. She sure was beautiful, but he hadn't been with another woman in many years, and it was going to take some getting used to. Sandy noticed that Rattler was uncomfortable. "Is everything OK? You don't have to tell me if you don't want to," Sandy assured.

"No, it's not that. I mean, that story is embarrassing, but that's not what's bothering me," Rattler replied.

"What is it?" Sandy asked, moving herself closer to Rattler. They were practically touching now.

Not knowing what to say and not being used to being in uncomfortable situations, Rattler replied, "It's just that I'm married."

"What? Oh!" Sandy said as she immediately began moving away.

"No, no—it's not what you think. I'm not that kind of guy. It's complicated." Rattler explained.

"What's so complicated about being married?" she asked.

As Rattler went about explaining the whole situation, he could feel himself becoming more comfortable with the reality of his relationship with his soon-to-be ex-wife. He was a good person and a hard-working guy who had chosen to go after a lifelong dream of becoming a naval aviator, and he was achieving his goals. He had no idea where his career or future would take him, but he did know that he didn't like being treated like crap when he would literally do anything for Jennifer. Well, he would have done anything… but that was in the past.

As Sandy listened to Rattler's story, she warmed up to him even more. *Who is this intriguing man?* He lived in a far-off land, doing a job that she didn't understand, but still, she couldn't help feeling attracted to him. When she was younger, she would have said that it was immaturity that had brought her to this rooftop with a stranger, but tonight, it was something more. All day and night, she waited on businessmen and high-powered people dressed in $10,000 suits, and it did nothing for her, but now, she was experiencing the first feelings of falling for a man in jeans and an AC/DC t-shirt. Granted, he was good-looking—very much so in an understated kind of way. He was the kind of guy who she could picture working on a farm, or coming into the house all dirty after fixing the car, and that pleased her. She'd grown up on a farm in Australia, and when she first became a flight attendant, all the glamour was appealing; now she longed for home.

As she drifted back into the conversation, Rattler was still trying to explain how he wasn't a bad guy for being with her on this rooftop when he was technically still married. Sandy smiled and did the one thing that she knew would finally shut him up. She leaned in and kissed him. They held the embrace for what seemed to be minutes, and the electricity it generated could have lit up the whole city. When Sandy finally did pull back, she could take it no longer. She grabbed Rattler's hand and led him off to her room.

"Wait! Don't you want to know how I got my call sign?" asked Rattler breathlessly.

"We'll have plenty of time for that later, honey."

CHAPTER 8

Staring out the window, watching the city fly by at extreme speeds, Rattler's head swayed back and forth as the cab driver weaved in and out of traffic. The driver had promised to get Rattler back to the ship quickly, but Rattler wouldn't have minded if he'd taken his time. Waking up next to a beautiful flight attendant only a few minutes earlier, Rattler had been told by the squadron duty officer (SDO) to get back to the ship. The *Nimitz* was pulling out of port as soon as everyone was on board; this was an immediate and emergency recall of personnel.

Rattler had been to his fair share of port calls at this point in his career, and he had never heard of such a recall. Initially, he thought that the duty officer was playing a joke on him, but when Clipper began banging on his hotel door, trying to wake him, it quickly became apparent that this was the real deal. When Rattler opened the door in his boxer shorts and Clipper put two and two together, Rattler's only response was that they would talk about it later. Clipper rarely exhibited that much urgency unless he was trying to get to a party or a woman; it was definitely not his habit to be in a hurry when leaving one or the other. Rattler got dressed quickly, explaining the situation to Sandy. She gave him her phone number and email, but Rattler suspected that she thought he was lying. *Well, if she hears something on the news about us in the upcoming days, then maybe she'll forgive me*, Rattler hoped.

"Don't for a minute think that you aren't going to fill me in on the full details of last night," Clipper said from the other side of the back seat.

"Sure, man—I'll fill you in. But first, what do you think this is all about?" Rattler asked.

"I'm sure it's nothing, man. Probably some drunk sailor got put in jail for hitting on a local and causing a fight, and we all have to pay the price," Clipper responded.

"I don't know, dude. I don't see CAG doing that—not a FULL recall of the whole ship. He knows how tightly wound everyone is, and cutting this port call short two days isn't going to help. I think something bigger is going on," Rattler said.

"Well, this probably isn't the best time to speculate," Clipper said, his eyes looking forward reminding Rattler that the cab driver could hear them.

Rattler hadn't thought about that. He remembered all the briefs about security before they got off the ship, and here he was talking about a full ship recall in front of a cab driver who could have less than desirable motives. Rattler thought back to his night with Sandy. She was completely different than his ex-wife in the sense that she listened to him and seemed to care about him and his needs. Rattler hadn't felt that kind of caring from a woman in a long time. For as long as he could remember, Jennifer had treated him poorly, but it wasn't like Rattler to give up.

His parents were still married after thirty-five years together. Sure, they had been through some ups and downs, but they never gave up; he respected that commitment and wanted to be the same way. That being said, when he'd received the email from Jennifer a few months ago saying she wanted a divorce, it hit him like a sack of bricks, knocking him back for a bit. However, Rattler was not going to beg, and eventually, he signed the paperwork—all while being deployed on an aircraft carrier in the middle of the ocean. On the positive side, he was able to surround himself with work and leave the emotional side of it for when he got home.

He began to piece together the circumstances of the last few months. At first, they were supposed to be doing a pure "West Pac" cruise with no intention of entering the Persian Gulf. That changed very quickly after they pulled out of San Diego Bay. Their deployment had been extended, and now they were being emergency recalled to the ship in the middle of their first decent port call. Rattler's mind began to race as to the cause for all this, but his questions would no doubt be answered soon.

The cab driver slid to a stop in front of the pier holding the USS *Nimitz.* As Rattler opened his door and Clipper paid the fare, Shotgun walked up with a clipboard and checked off their names. The pier was a mess of people trying to get back to the ship and those working to bring provisions onboard for an immediate pull out. Rattler noticed that all of the radar antennas on the bridge were already spinning and that the tug boats were waiting to help ease the *Nimitz* out to sea. Something was definitely up.

"Thanks for getting back so soon, guys. I know this is a pain," Shotgun said to them.

"What's going on, man? Do you know how much fun I was having when you called? This better be important!" Clipper returned.

"I'm sure we'll all hear about your good times in detail, Clipper, but I assure you that this is a big deal. Skipper and XO are currently in a brief with CAG and the admiral, and we have an all-officers meeting at 1900," Shotgun informed them.

Clipper looked at his watch and immediately noted how little time he would have to sleep off his hangover. Rattler asked, "What do you need from us, Shotgun? How can we help?"

"I think we're good. I only have a few other people to find, and then we are all accounted for. I would suggest that you go to your divisions and talk with the chiefs. Make sure no one is calling home or emailing home to give any of this info away. We were told to keep this under wraps as much as possible. I doubt the email is even working on the ship right now anyway. Other than that, get to the meeting later today and be ready to fly or stand alerts tonight," Shotgun replied.

"You got it. Let us know if anything comes up," Rattler said as he grabbed his bag and followed Clipper up to the ship. "Still think this is because of a drunken bar fight?" Rattler asked Clipper.

"No man, something's up… something big," Clipper responded.

Chapter 9

Hangovers seemed worse on the ship. Whether it was the noise or the smell or just the close quarters, Rattler never liked the first day out of port trying to adjust to life back at sea. Unable to sleep, he sat at his desk in his stateroom, playing with the piece of paper containing Sandy's number and email. He let his mind dream about this beautiful woman.

Rattler was a hopeless romantic, and he quickly began trying to figure out how it could work between them. He was an American and constantly deployed, and she lived in Australia. But his orders would be up eventually, and then he would be assigned a shore tour, most likely as a flight instructor. Maybe that would allow him to see her? Or maybe he could apply for a joint training tour in Australia … just as his mind went there, reality pushed back. Throwing the piece of paper in his desk locker, he looked at his watch: 1830—time to wake up Clipper. He had been sleeping since they got back to the ship, and Rattler didn't want him to miss the meeting.

"Yo, man, wake up," Rattler said, lightly tapping on the side of Clipper's rack. With a little more persuasion, Clipper finally roared to life with a huge burp.

"Always the officer and the gentleman," Rattler remarked.

"Did I miss the meeting?" Clipper asked.

"No, man. It's in twenty minutes…want to get some food first?" Rattler asked.

"No, let's just go and we can eat afterward," Clipper replied, a decision they would come to regret.

The ship had set off from the pier only thirty minutes after Clipper and Rattler reported back. It had been running full speed toward somewhere ever since. A modern US aircraft carrier is said to be able to go thirty-plus knots. As they walked to the secure part of the ship for the meeting, Rattler thought they must be using all of the "plus" today.

As they entered the small, secure briefing space, Rattler noticed that the majority of the squadron was already there. While most of the new guys stood, there were still two chairs available in the back. Rattler smiled as he thought about the hierarchy of a squadron at sea. New guys knew better than to sit in the back (those were the "cooler" seats, away from the skipper and XO where the more senior JOs would want to sit). He liked this place and the people in this squadron. With all that was going on at home, Rattler decided that, if asked, he would gladly extend his tour, especially for an extra six months while Clipper was still here.

"Attention on deck!" someone yelled. Everyone immediately stopped talking and stood up at attention.

"Seats," CAG said matter-of-factly as he strolled into the room. Captain Jeffery "Nails" Grogan, or "CAG" as he was known, was a career navy man. Rattler noticed that the man commanded immediate respect. CAG was a career fighter pilot, the kind every pilot looked up to. With many deployments under his belt, a perfect family at home, and not one, but two successful skipper tours—the last of which was at the Navy Fighter Weapons School or TOPGUN—CAG had been selected to run this air wing. Often described as a man who you wanted on your side and never wanted to cross, CAG cared about his people and looked after each person as he would a family member. Of course, if you crossed him, he would rule you with an iron fist, but he would manage to do so in a somewhat caring way.

"Listen up: I'm going to make this quick. Nothing I say here is to be repeated in a phone call or email. And God help you if I find out anyone here disobeys that order. Last night, I was called by CENTCOM and told to recall all personnel to the *Nimitz.* Of course I asked why, and he explained that tensions in the Persian Gulf were heating up again. An oil rig that was controlled by a US company, with protection from US contract forces, came under siege last night and was taken over. Reports show at least five dead and more injured. Our intelligence tells us that the group is Al Qaeda and that they plan to use the platform for one of two things. First, set it on fire to show their power in the region, or second, as a missile platform to attack ships coming and going to the port in Bahrain. Either way, the Al Qaeda group knew that there were Americans on board when they attacked, so they made it our problem.

"Leave no doubt, ladies and gentlemen—I do not care that the people on that platform are not members of the military: we will protect them at all costs. All of those security forces are made up of veterans, and I personally know one of them. I'm trying to get in contact for more intel. As we speak, a SEAL Team is prepping an attack for 2300 tonight. They will have their own helo air support, and we will support them. I have instructed the Hornet squadrons to prep teams and man alerts and come up with a tanker plan. Ladies and gentlemen, I expect that there will be a Hawkeye airborne constantly throughout this attack providing command and control—"

"You can count on it, sir!" Skipper interrupted.

With that, CAG shot Skipper a look that could have frozen water, and continued. "I know you have had recent maintenance problems, but I expect you will figure out how to cover this tasking. Let us be clear: this is a real-world mission and what we have trained for. I will not ask you to do anything that I would not do myself. I will put you in harm's way, but I will be there with you. If anyone is not comfortable with this, speak up now." CAG paused and there was not a sound. "Very well, that is all." He walked to the door, pausing after a few steps.

"Rattler, come see me in my stateroom in twenty minutes."

"Yes, sir," Rattler replied. He could feel everyone's eyes on him.

CAG continued to the door. "Attention on deck!" someone yelled.

"Carry on," CAG stated as he exited the room.

At the back of the room, Clipper and Rattler's eyes met as the noise level of everyone talking and barking orders began to rise. "Definitely not a drunken sailor," Clipper said.

"Nope," Rattler replied.

CHAPTER 10

Being called to CAG's stateroom was completely unexpected. About a week ago, Grins had told Rattler that CAG wanted to talk to him about the close-call flight, so Rattler was expecting that. Of course, no one else in the whole officer's meeting seemed to know what was going on, including Skipper. As he approached the door to CAG's stateroom, Rattler wondered what it would be like. For all officers on board an aircraft carrier, their stateroom doubled as their office. The higher the rank, the bigger and nicer the accommodation (along with fewer roommates involved). Once you reached CAG's level, your stateroom was actually two adjoining rooms: one for sleeping and one for work. As he approached the door and knocked on it, Rattler took a deep breath.

"ENTER!" barked CAG from inside.

As Rattler opened the door and entered, he stood at attention in front of CAG's desk and tried not to be shocked at the superior condition of the room.

"Sir, LT Jack Owen reporting as—"

"Sit!" CAG barked before Rattler could finish his sentence. Rattler moved to a chair in front of CAG's massive desk and sat at attention.

"Rattler," CAG began, "I am going to get to the point because we both have a lot of work to do. That landing you made the other night was nothing short of heroic, and I do not use that term lightly. I have spoken to your maintenance officer, and that aircraft was on the verge of unflyable. He said that given a 10,000-ft runway back at PT Mugu, most pilots would have still ended up with a mishap, yet somehow, you put it down on a postage stamp in bad weather in the middle of the Persian

Gulf. That was an extremely risky maneuver and could have cost a lot of people their lives. What do you have to say for yourself?"

Rattler was immediately taken aback and felt like he needed to be on the defensive. This was the first time that someone wasn't praising him for his actions, and he'd half thought that was the purpose of this meeting. Now, with no time to mentally prepare, he replied, "Sir, when we first got the indication of low hydraulic pressure, I went through the checklist, but in the back of my mind, I figured that it was just a frozen gauge. I know you are familiar with the problems the E-2C has with this happening at higher colder altitudes. At that time, I made up my mind to come back to the ship, and the guys in the back coordinated for our immediate recovery. I was hoping to get it on deck before the second system was lost. It wasn't until we were on final that I realized more was wrong with the aircraft because it was getting hard to control."

"So, why not just fly upwind and bail out? Give it back to the tax-payers," CAG interrupted.

"Sir, with all due respect, I was trained to fly the E-2C by the best. I am an aircraft commander, and have almost 1,000 hours in this plane. I felt that I could land it and give my crew a better chance at survival. I briefed everyone and instructed them to go over the bailout procedures on final. I told them that if it got too bad, I would fly it upwind and let them bail out. I would then ditch it ahead of the ship," Rattler replied, feeling completely defensive and uncomfortable now.

"Ditch! Do you think you would have survived a ditching in that aircraft?" CAG asked.

"Sir—honestly, no. But that was not my first concern at the time. The safety of my crew, the individuals on the flight deck, and my aircraft were all at the forefront of my mind. What would happen to me was an afterthought," Rattler replied.

"Exactly! That's why I called you in here. Rattler, I am in charge of over 100 aviators in this air wing flying five different types of aircraft, and they are the best. I expect them to be; I require it. But some are not. Some care more about themselves or question the reason we are out here;

they question the long deployments away from home. I know that your wife has asked you for a divorce."

Rattler's eyes opened wide now. *How could CAG, who is in charge of so much, know that? Who told him?*

"I'm sorry for that," CAG continued. "Some women aren't cut out for this life. I'm not going to sugarcoat it: it sucks at times. But we do what we need to do for our country, our loved ones at home, and most importantly, the men and women flying next to us out here on the *Nimitz.* You have shown great courage in how you handled that situation. You are one of my LSO team leads, and with that, there is immense responsibility on your shoulders to get the planes safely back aboard regardless of the weather and sea conditions.

"And because you handled that responsibility so well, I am having you fly the first Hawkeye tonight in support of the rescue mission. Your XO is med down right now with an ear infection, so who do you want to fly with? And before you answer, know that you will launch first; I will ask you to stay airborne for as long as possible—with very little fuel to get back to the ship—and as soon as you launch, you will be in a SAM WEZ from that oil platform that can reach out to you well above the max altitude of the Hawkeye. You will be asked to fly the Hawkeye on perfect mission profile, in an extremely dangerous environment, in order to allow the NFOs in the back to provide the command and control to make this mission a success. So, who is it going to be?" CAG asked.

Rattler had been hanging on every word and just now realized that he had begun to sweat. He had trained for this, but training and real life are different. He knew the threat was there when flying over Iraq or Afghanistan for a surface-to-air missile, but he also knew the likelihood of attack was very slim. But this was different: tonight, he would have to call on all his training, skill, and luck to pull off the mission. He also knew that having the right person next to him, one with nerves of steel and the ability to stay calm under pressure, was vital to accomplishing what they were being asked to do. There was only one answer to CAG's question.

"Clipper, sir. I would like Clipper to be my copilot tonight," Rattler replied.

"I figured you would say that. He looked a little rough in the meeting… Do you think he's had time to sleep off the port call?"

"Yes, sir. But honestly, even if he hadn't, I would take him over anyone else, even after a port call," Rattler replied, bringing a smile to CAG's face.

"OK. You and Clipper will launch ahead of the air wing. Go tell him to take a cold shower, and then go down and meet with the strike planning team and intelligence officer to get a handle on that SAM threat," CAG directed. Rattler stood up to leave. "Let me know if you need anything else, and know, son, that I will be launching the first wave and leading the strike, so I need your best to protect my six."

"Yes, sir!" Rattler replied and then immediately thought of something else he would like, but hesitated in asking for it. CAG sensed that something was on his mind and pressed Rattler for what it was. "Sir, is there any chance of knowing who will be the mission commander for tonight's flight? It's just that some crews work better together than others, and—"

"You don't want your skipper back there, I get it," CAG interrupted. "He has been assigned to shipboard duty tonight, and although he is not very happy about it, he will obey. Your mission commander for tonight will be Shotgun. He is already down with the rest of the crew in strike planning. Now, go wake up Clipper and tell him to drink some coffee. I'll see you in the brief," CAG finished as Rattler smiled and exited the stateroom.

Rattler knew it was a longshot to not have Skipper in the back of the plane for such an important mission, but it just showed how little respect the guy commanded. Rattler felt good as he walked through the passageways to his stateroom to find Clipper. This is what he trained for: all those years in flight school had led up to this. It was time to see if he could really hack it.

CHAPTER 11

"Takeoff checks complete," Clipper said from the right seat of the Hawkeye as they sat on the bow catapult, waiting for launch.

"Radar is up, link is up, good comms with 'Shocker 501,' and we are all set back here," Shotgun confirmed. Shocker 501 would be flying relatively close by and would provide enemy radar jamming along with a ton of other things that would help Rattler stay out of the enemy's gunsights.

"Do you think what CAG said is true?" Clipper asked Rattler, referring to CAG's comment in the brief about not being able to take out the SAM on the oil platform with a bomb since it would also kill the people they were trying to rescue.

"I guess so, man; I mean, it makes sense. If we bomb it, then this mission is kind of pointless. I'm sure Shocker will do their job, and this will be another routine flight, just killing time before we hit MIDRATS," Rattler replied, half trying to convince himself.

"I sure hope so," Clipper replied, sounding unusually concerned.

The plan was to launch the E-2C Hawkeye and the EA-6B Prowler. The prowler would jam the enemy and hopefully keep the Hawkeye out of sight while the Hawkeye provided vital command and control. There were so many players involved, from this air wing, to other surface ships, Navy SEALs, and even a submarine in the Persian Gulf. If all went as planned, which Rattler hoped it would, then the SEALs would launch from the submarine and take control of the oil platform before the enemy even knew what hit them. If it went that way, then all that Rattler and Clipper would have to worry about were the standard threats associated with nighttime carrier operations.

On the other hand, if the enemy knew the SEALs were coming, they would most likely kill their hostages and launch as many surface-to-air missiles (SAMs) as they could before the SEALs arrived. Intel reported a reload rate of three minutes for the type of SAM they believed was on the oil platform, and they also believed the likely target would be the easiest to hit and the one that would cause the most confusion to the battle space, a.k.a. the E-2C Hawkeye currently sitting on the bow catapult, waiting to launch.

"Hey, I need your 'A' game tonight, brother! Where's that natural swagger I'm so used to? Let's pretend we aren't about to launch into the night skies above the Persian Gulf. How about we pretend we're back in Ventura, California, and it's a typical Saturday night. Clipper's on the prowl for some young, dumb, and most likely too-liberal-for-their-own-good women to show us a good time," Rattler suggested.

"Wouldn't that be nice." Clipper leaned back in his seat and closed his eyes. A smile crept across his face.

As Rattler looked outside, he saw a lot of activity as the launch was about to begin. He slowly advanced the power levers to move the Hawkeye forward and over the shuttle. He held the brakes and waited for the signal from the flight deck crew to run up the engines.

"All right, guys, we are about out of here. Remember to wait until we're far enough away from the ship before we turn on any of the systems," Rattler reminded.

"Copy," Shotgun said from the back as Clipper shot him a thumbs up from his seat in the cockpit.

They were launching under EMCON procedures in the hope of keeping the enemy guessing to where the carrier was located; unless they had an emergency, they would not make any communication after launch. Once outside the designated ring, they would turn on all systems and essentially pop up on the radar. Of course, the goal was to have Shocker 501 already working so that they would never actually pop up. The shooter took over now on the flight deck, and after some checks, gave Rattler the "run-up" signal. Rattler immediately took his eyes off him and ran the power up to full, clenching the catapult grip in his right hand. With his left hand, he did a full wipe out of the control surfaces twice, checking for anything wrong. His eyes scanned all the gauges to make sure the engines were operating as they should, which they were.

"Looks good... You like it?" Rattler asked Clipper.

"Let's get this over with, man," Clipper replied.

Rattler took one deep breath and with the pinky on his right hand, he flicked the switch that turned on the Hawkeye's exterior lights—the signal to the shooter that he was ready. Time stood still as the shooter looked forward and aft to check the Hawkeye and its flight path one last time. Then, he squatted down and touched the deck. Inside the right catwalk stood a young airman not completely aware of why tonight was different, but he knew something was happening. He had one goal: to make sure he did not screw anything up. For the last ten minutes, he'd been standing in front of a big red button, hands in the air above his head, staring at the shooter and waiting for the signal. Once he saw it, he knew what to do. With one last look forward and aft for safety, he lowered one hand down, pushing the button, and then immediately returning it to its previous position.

Mere seconds had elapsed since Rattler turned on the lights, but it felt like an eternity, especially tonight. With the Hawkeye shaking under full power in the dark night, the tension of the mission weighed on Rattler's mind, almost to the point of wondering why it was taking so long. Just as he was about to take his eyes off the instrument panel, he was shoved back into his seat by a force four times that of gravity.

"Good shot," Rattler said over the ICS as the Hawkeye rocketed to a speed of 150 knots in just under two seconds, lifting off of the flight deck and becoming airborne.

Chapter 12

"Damn quiet tonight," Clipper remarked from the right seat of the Hawkeye.

"Yeah, almost too quiet," Rattler replied as he climbed the E-2C Hawkeye to an altitude of 29,000 feet. That would be their mission profile altitude for tonight's flight. It would allow the NFOs in the back a good, stable platform and also allow Rattler to save enough fuel to be airborne as long as possible. As the aircraft climbed, Rattler noticed how clear the skies were: no moon, but no clouds either. It was rare for the Persian Gulf to look like this. Rattler had learned early on that constant scanning was the key to being a good pilot. Keep your eyes moving and you notice things. So, he was doing just that: checking over the gauges, looking outside the aircraft, and occasionally looking over at Clipper who seemed to be doing the same thing. *Don't stagnate or get comfortable;* that's when bad things happened.

"Shocker 501 has us in sight and says we can go midnight," Shotgun called from the back.

"Roger, going dark," Rattler replied as he shut off the exterior lights and dimmed all the interior lights to the minimum setting. This step would make them harder to see for anyone who was looking. Since intel on the SAM on the oil platform was not complete, they did not know if it was radar guided or visually guided, but by going dark, it would be harder to take a shot at them.

"Have you thought about what you are going to do if they launch that thing?" Clipper asked, breaking the silence.

"Of course I have," Rattler replied, but in truth he hadn't. In his mind, he thought that the likelihood of someone shooting at them was extremely low, even with the location of their airborne station to the oil platform.

"Care to share your plan with me?" Clipper joked.

"Well, I am going to fly, make the plane's movements unpredictable, keep the missile in sight, and make the tracking solution as difficult as I can," Rattler answered.

"So you *haven't* thought about it… How about you just do some pilot shit?" Clipper replied with a smile.

"Right…some pilot shit!" Rattler answered, looking over at his friend and copilot.

"All right, let's see if these work." Clipper donned a special set of night-vision goggles (NVGs) that had been designed to be tested in the Hawkeye. When the aircraft was originally built by Grumman, no one thought that they would need to fly around using NVGs like the fighter pilots do, but Rattler and Clipper had been using them just to see if it would help their overall situational awareness. So far, it had been a success. For this mission, they were using new helmet clips that would actually allow them to attach the NVGs for hands-off use, just like their fighter brethren.

"Sure does open your eyes," Rattler said after adjusting his world to a greenish hue. He could see everything, even if his depth perception was off. He scanned the horizon for other planes and saw Shocker 501 exactly where it should be, completely lights out, but no doubt inside working all their systems to jam any enemy radar and communications. Things seemed peaceful as Rattler scanned around and got used to flying while wearing the goggles. The E-2C was on autopilot, but he wanted to be able to fly with the NVGs if needed, so he just sat there, getting accustomed to them.

"Is that the platform?" Clipper asked as he peered over the nose of the plane.

Rattler followed his gaze and then checked their position. "Must be," he replied.

"Well now, that is freaking cool, man... If nothing else, we are going to get a front row seat for the fireworks when those SEALs send those assholes to meet their maker," Clipper said, feeling patriotic.

"D-10," Shotgun said from the back, letting the crew know that the SEALs would be making their final approach and would attack the oil platform in ten minutes.

Everyone had their own duties at this point in the flight. Shotgun was busy with the other two NFOs in the back, making sure the radar worked perfectly and coordinating all the efforts between the *Nimitz* and the SEALs. Rattler had decided in the brief that it would be better if everyone didn't listen to the attack radio because he needed people to focus on their jobs. That left Shotgun, as the overall mission commander, to give updates to the rest of the crew, which was fine with him. Shotgun was a consummate professional who rarely made mistakes. He was a definite must for this mission if they wanted it to go off without a hitch, and he was living up to expectations. This was the type of mission that would propel Shotgun's career into fast-forward mode. Next, he would take command of a squadron and then he would probably become a CAG himself. Rattler thought about how he wouldn't mind being in Shotgun's squadron in the future.

"D-5, they are in attack mode. We are green light," Shotgun announced.

Rattler and Clipper leaned forward to see the oil platform as if they were trying to actually see the SEALs make their approach, but that wasn't going to happen: the Hawkeye was too far away, and the SEALs were too good at not being seen. Minutes seemed to hang on each other, and time slowed as Rattler felt his heart rate begin to rise. His eyes constantly scanned the area, and he would occasionally switch radios to keep on top of the chatter, but everyone was quiet now. They had a job to do and talking about it wasn't going to get it done. Rattler envied those Navy SEALs and their chance to see some real action. He'd always wondered how he would react if tested in combat. So far, he'd proven that he could handle bad weather and broken planes, he imagined that if someone was shooting at him, that would be a whole different world.

"Touchdown!" Shotgun called from the back, indicating that the assault had been a success. Rattler knew that his aircraft would be the last to recover aboard the *Nimitz,* so he was in no hurry to leave station. A short while later, Shotgun came back up on the ICS. "Looks like all went according to plan. The SEALs are finishing up their sweep of the platform and have all hostages secure. They just need to finish up and make sure there are no more tangos on board and then we are done here, boys. Nice work!" he said excitedly.

"602, 501 on your tac," called the pilot of Shocker 501.

"Go ahead," Clipper replied.

"Looks like our work is done here for tonight. Request permission to break formation and head back to the ship."

"Cleared off, man. Safe landing," Clipper replied. He had calmed down a lot since the launch from the ship and was probably going through the same thought process that Rattler was. He was happy the mission had been a success. It sounded like no one had been hurt either. All in all, it was just another boring night in the skies above the Persian Gulf.

Shotgun called Rattler. "We are done here, buddy. Let's head home."

"You got it—coming off station," Rattler replied.

"Hey how about a three wire tonight?" Shotgun joked.

"For you? Anything," Rattler replied.

As Rattler began to turn the plane toward the ship, he kept his NVGs on because he wanted to practice using them some more. Clicking off the autopilot, he began a right-hand turn as Clipper was taking his NVGs off for the recovery and stowing them in his helmet bag. Taking a look at the oil platform one last time, Rattler saw something out of the corner of his eye.

"SHIT! Did you see that?" Rattler screamed to Clipper.

"Huh? What?" Clipper replied, looking up quickly.

"Something just launched off the oil platform. It's… I think, maybe it's… Shit, it is! MISSILE airborne!" Rattler confirmed to the entire crew. He immediately heard back from Shocker.

"SAM launch, SAM launch… Bearing 180 from our position; not tracking us. Rattler—you have it?"

Rattler didn't have time to reply. He was busy keeping the missile in sight. He knew as soon as the missile's burner ran out of gas, it would be even harder to see. "Bro, watch my numbers," Rattler said to Clipper. He needed his copilot to watch the gauges and make sure he didn't get too low or slow.

"Everyone, strap in NOW!" Clipper said over the ICS.

Rattler turned the plane back toward the platform in the hope of making it easier to see the missile, which it was. He was already descending and building up the airspeed he would need if this thing kept tracking them. His heartbeat was off the charts now, and every ounce of his body was alive flying the plane. Just minutes ago, Rattler had been thinking about his upcoming landing and what he was going to eat once back on the ship, and now he was fighting for his life and the lives of his crew.

But through it all, he was calm. The missile continued to guide onto the Hawkeye as Rattler followed its course through the night sky. Rattler was the only one who could see it because without the NVGs, the SAM was invisible. Time froze as the missile continued to track them; all the while, Rattler hoped like hell that it would veer off course. Because the Hawkeye wasn't equipped with any countermeasures, like chaff or flares that could be launched to trick the missile, there wasn't much he could do. His only option was to keep the missile in sight, and at the last second, aggressively maneuver the Hawkeye out of its path and hope it missed.

"Hang on, guys… This is going to get rough," Rattler warned over the ICS while never taking his eyes off the missile. "Stand by for impact in 10."

With the missile definitely tracking his aircraft, he started counting in his head. *NINE…I am the only one who can save this crew and plane. EIGHT…They are counting on me. SEVEN…I have been trained for this. SIX… What will my mom do if this goes badly? FIVE…It's tracking now and getting bigger, just off our left side. FOUR…Damn the sonofabitch who launched this thing. THREE…Hopefully the E-2C can handle what's about to happen. TWO…Hang on…NOW!* Rattler jammed the yoke full forward and rolled into the missile, hoping any damage would impact the top of the plane and not the vital engines or hydraulic systems: he needed his flight controls intact. Time stood still once again as Rattler watched the missile travel down the left side of the plane. With his neck strained to the left, he saw the moment it exploded—completely blinding him.

CHAPTER 13

The impact of the missile shook the Hawkeye sideways, and the aircraft seemed to groan as if in pain as the shrapnel from the SAM pierced its skin. Rattler was momentarily blinded, but his hands were still trying to fly the plane. For a second, he thought that he *was* actually blind until he remembered the NVGs. He reached up and ripped them off his helmet, trying to get his eyes to work. Clipper was yelling something at him, but he couldn't hear it. It was like a dream.

"BRO! We have to shut down the left!" Clipper screamed, reaching for the left propeller lever and pulling it to the feather position.

"It feathered!!" Rattler replied, or at least what was left of it did. Straining to look outside, Rattler could see that four of the eight propeller blades were gone, the engine was completely shot, and the window on the left side of the cockpit was cracked. He was able to get the aircraft under control and begin an emergency descent in case the window didn't hold. His eyes went back to scanning.

"Give it to me, man…one by one. How are our systems?" Rattler asked Clipper.

"Left engine is done; right looks good. We lost one hydraulic system, but the other seems to be holding. Lights and radios seem to be working OK," Clipper reported. "How are the flight controls?"

"Seem OK for now. Turning back toward the ship," Rattler replied as he brought everyone up on the ICS. "Shotgun, we are down to one engine and one hydraulic system. Give me a report on what you see back there."

"Copy. It's pretty bad. All systems are down, but we are trying to get at least one scope back up. There was a small fire, but that is out. I will keep an eye on it, but we need to get back to the ship ASAP!"

"Copy that, buddy. On our way!" Rattler replied.

Rattler began the descent to a lower altitude while Clipper got the ship on the radio and discussed a plan. Initially, it looked like CAG was leaning toward a bailout, but Clipper convinced him that they could get the plane on board. This was a lofty goal: to the best of Clipper's knowledge, a Hawkeye had never been hit with a SAM before, so once again, Rattler and Clipper were essentially test pilots. They hoped that Grumman Iron Works would come through one more time and keep the Hawkeye from falling apart.

"Set up for ten miles behind the ship, bro. I can run the checklists fast and get configured, but I want just a little more time in case I have to blow the gear down," Clipper said to Rattler.

Both looked at each other and the same thought crossed their minds—would the gear come down? If not, that was it… CAG would have them bail out, and the plane would be a loss. No time to think about it now though. *Bucket of luck, bucket of skill*, Rattler thought.

Rattler had to use all his skills to keep the stricken Hawkeye airborne long enough to even have a chance of landing on the ship. Clipper was diligently running through checklists and ensuring they would be ready once their time came. Everything seemed to speed up once they were at the ten-mile mark, behind the ship on a straight-in approach. Rattler had been in this situation before, but at least this time the weather was cooperating. The landing gear did come down, and after being configured for landing, Rattler asked for the landing checklist.

"Landing gear?"

"Three down and locked."

"Flaps?"

"Full."

"Hook?"

"Down."

"Landing checks complete," Clipper responded.

Over ICS Rattler talked to everyone. "OK guys, things could get bumpy here. Hang on and be prepared to get out of the plane as soon as we come to a stop."

"600, Hawkeye ball, 4.6," Rattler called over the radio.

"Roger ball," the LSO replied.

"Right engine is on fire," Clipper said as calmly as he could.

"What?" Rattler fired back, momentarily taking his eyes off the ship.

"Got a fire light on the right, brother. Think we should let it burn?" Clipper asked.

"Little power," called the LSO.

"Yea, screw it. Let it burn. Let's land this thing. Everyone be ready to evacuate as soon as we stop; watch for spinning props!" Rattler called to everyone.

Instinctively, Rattler had said to watch for the props, but the left motor barely had any props left, and they hadn't been spinning for quite a while. The right motor was on fire and who knew if it would even be there when they finally touched down. But it didn't matter now. He had to fly the best landing of his life and could only hope that the E2 would hold together. Rattler's hands and feet worked in unison to counter the nose pitching up and down while he also tried to stay on the perfect three-degree glide path to a ship that was moving away from them. Rattler's grip on the yoke and throttles tightened even though he told himself to calm down. With the red "FIRE" light glaring at him, he focused all of his concentration on the landing until the second the E2's wheels hit the deck and the arresting hook grabbed the wire.

Almost immediately, Clipper said, "I'm shutting down the right."

Rattler replied, "Do it. Everyone get out of the plane. The right side is on fire; go out the main door."

"Sir, 600 shutting down in the landing area, engine fire on the right side, parking brake set," Rattler calmly said over the radio. Clipper was already out of his seat and heading to the door. In a moment of complete calmness, Rattler realized that he'd done it again. His luck bucket wasn't quite as empty, or maybe his skill bucket was a bit fuller. He knew at that instant that his career was about to change: being the only Hawkeye pilot to ever get shot by a SAM and to survive to talk about it was sheer bliss. He thought about the crew—Clipper was single, and he was about to be single himself—but all the guys in back had wives and kids, and the gravity of how close they'd come to being widows and orphans immediately hit him…or maybe it had been Clipper.

"Dude, get the fuck out of here!" Clipper yelled as he slapped Rattler's shoulder and made sure that his buddy started moving toward the door.

After unstrapping, Rattler got up, grabbed his helmet bag, and moved quickly to the door. There was an odd absence of sound until he hit the fresh air outside and could immediately smell the fire and hear the pandemonium on the flight deck. Firefighters were working hard to put out the fire, while others were running around, towing planes away from the Hawkeye and trying to minimize the damage. As all of this was going on, Rattler stood frozen to the spot, not sure what to do—that is, until the contents of his last meal decided it was time to make another appearance.

"Easy, buddy," Rattler heard as he tried to stand back up. Looking over he saw Spool, his XO who had come to meet him. "Really nice job out there; that plane gave you all she had."

"Yes, sir," Rattler replied.

"How about we get you inside and out of your flight gear?" Spool said as he motioned for Rattler to head toward the entrance to the tower of the ship. Rattler glanced back to make sure the flight deck crews didn't need anything; they seemed to just be monitoring the plane now that the fire was out. He began walking to the tower, still in a daze.

"Rattler!" Spool said as Rattler turned around. "Mission success! Shit hot job, man!"

Rattler nodded. *Mission success.*

Chapter 14

The days following the mission were a complete blur. Rattler spent countless hours debriefing the with both the intelligence officers, plus CAG and his staff while everyone tried to figure out how the terrorists got off that lucky shot. Additionally, Rattler spent hours on a video teleconference with staff members at TOPGUN back in Fallon, Nevada, trying to come up with what worked and what could have worked better for an E-2C Hawkeye defense against a SAM; they were truly in uncharted waters there.

In between all the meetings, life on the ship became more and more routine, as it always did. The NFOs from aircraft 600 were cleared to fly again, and rumor had it that they were all being put in for air medals for their work on the mission. Rattler and Clipper were scheduled for their mishap board the next day, but from everything he was hearing, it sounded like a formality. Rattler was hoping to get airborne again soon.

He had become a little bit of a local star on the ship with his maintenance department too. Whenever he walked through the hangar bay and one of his line division guys or girls saw him, they wanted a photo with him next to 600. This happened daily because Rattler would spend a little time down there each day. He felt a bond with the plane that had literally given its all to get them back to the ship safely. Immediately following the mishap, word was that aircraft 600 would be pushed overboard since it looked like a total loss. But days later, she still sat here in the hangar in a state of disrepair, looking like a bloodied warrior with no home.

"She's going to TOPGUN," Shotgun said to Rattler who found himself daydreaming next to the aircraft.

"Huh?" Rattler replied.

"I guess they want to study it. It was confirmed this morning that this is the first E-2C Hawkeye to be hit by a SAM, and it survived! So, reps from Grumman will be here later in the week. After they study the aircraft, it will be wrapped up and kept here until we pull into San Diego. Then the navy will figure out how to get it Fallon so they can study it and hopefully come up with better tactics for the future."

"Wow that's pretty intense," Rattler commented, trying to process what Shotgun was telling him.

"Yeah, definitely is. Make no mistake—what you did up there the other night was nothing short of heroic. The news has spread through the entire navy; you are the talk of the town. My wife and I have set up a set of code words in emails to help keep in touch over these deployments, but no code words were needed for what she told me in the last email. She said if our daughter was older, she would set you two up!"

"Thanks for that, but I'm going to stay single for now," Rattler laughed. "I'm just glad we had the crew that we did to get that job done. What I did was just a small part of the bigger picture, and I couldn't have done it without you guys."

"Sometimes you are too humble for your own good. I'll catch up with you later. I've got to talk to Chief about our plan for finishing the deployment with only three Hawkeyes," Shotgun said as he walked off to his meeting.

Rattler went back to his thoughts as Shotgun walked away. The chain of events over the past few months was truly unreal for anyone's life, but why him? His goals of being a navy aviator and living in this demanding world had seemed far-fetched when he was younger, but now that he was living it, he couldn't believe it. He tried to live by the words CAG said to him once: "Never read your own press." Basically, the message was to stay grounded, work hard, and not get caught up with what others were saying about your accomplishments. Just keep your head down and keep working hard—that was the only way to be successful. Rattler knew that such advice was invaluable. He just hoped that he could keep heeding those words amidst all that was happening in his life.

CHAPTER 15

Rattler headed up to the ready room, hoping to find a computer to check his email. To his surprise, the ready room was virtually empty, which was rare. Spike was on duty and dealing with some paperwork while the TV at the front of the room carried video feed from the flight deck. Rattler thought it would be a good time to catch up on work and see if he'd received any emails from home. As he sat down to log onto the computer, Clipper walked in.

"Hey brother, how are things?"

"Same ole, same ole, man. When do you think we'll fly again?" Rattler replied.

"After tomorrow morning, once we get this mishap board behind us. I wouldn't be surprised if we fly tomorrow night—have to keep up our night currency aboard the ship, you know," Clipper joked.

Rattler half laughed as he scanned the emails piling up in his inbox. There were the usual messages from friends back home, some work-related emails from his chief, and a couple of notes from his parents. He'd been putting off writing them back because he missed them a lot. Life at sea wasn't easy, and he found himself daydreaming of fishing trips with his dad as a kid. If he closed his eyes, he could see his dad at the wheel of his thirty-five-foot fishing boat, wearing a huge smile on his face and exuding the confidence of someone who was truly comfortable in his surroundings. Even as a kid, Rattler recognized and admired his father for that.

His father was the kind of man who would always take care of his family, no matter what. He worked his fingers to the bone, rising before the sun and returning home long after Rattler had gone to sleep. To

Rattler, it often seemed like he didn't see his dad for weeks. While Rattler spent a lot of time at the automotive garage with his family, he was just a stupid kid who acted like he didn't want to be there; he certainly gave his father some grief. But now, as a grown man, Rattler would give anything to be home and working on cars with his dad. He longed for the simpler times when he'd felt like he was in control. His last flight in 600 revealed to him his own mortality, and while it wasn't the first time a Hawkeye had shown him that, this time was different. He could not blame it on faulty maintenance or bad weather: this time, there had been someone out there trying to kill him. This time, it felt much more personal.

"We're getting another Dubai," Clipper said.

"Huh?" Rattler replied, shaken from his daydream.

"That's the rumor on the LSO platform today. CAG and the skipper are working another Dubai since the last one was cut short, and things have gotten a little crazy around here," Clipper explained.

"Well, that would be cool," Rattler answered.

"Especially if Sandy and Cheri can make it in." Clipper joked as he stood up. "I need to get my uniform ready for tomorrow and get some sleep, brother. Don't let your demons haunt you, man. You flew the shit out of that plane the other night, and you need to walk into tomorrow with that same swagger. Nothing can touch you, remember that. I'll see you downstairs."

"Thanks, brother. Wouldn't be here without you. See you in a bit," Rattler replied as he went back to his email. Three emails in particular caught his attention: one from Sandy (he would have to read that later) one from Jennifer, his soon to be ex-wife, and one from an email address he did not recognize. He opened the one from Jennifer first.

"Jack, honey, we need to talk soon. Rumors of what happened on your ship have reached us here, and it sounds like you were heroic. That is the kind of man I want to be with. I miss you so much. I know that I have strayed, but I didn't realize the man you were. If this story is true, you have become very sexy in my eyes. If the story is not true, then I am sorry to bother you, and I hope you are safe. Love Jennifer."

Rattler let out a sigh as he rubbed his eyes. Spike looked over at him.

"Everything OK, buddy?" Spike asked.

"Yeah, man—just women, you know?" Rattler replied.

"The cause of and solution to all of life's problems my friend." Spike laughed.

Rattler moved on to the last email. He did not recognize the sender, but it was from a ship's email account, so he opened it. As soon as he clicked on the email, it opened in a new window, which Rattler thought was odd since the other emails did not do that.

"There is more to things than what appears on the surface. A/C 600's fate is much more than meets the eye." Rattler read in silence, and as soon as he finished, the email disappeared. He went to look in his inbox again, and it was gone. He searched all folders, including the trash, and there was nothing. Just as Rattler started to think that he was losing his mind, Spike mentioned that he was getting ready to lock up the ready room for the night to get some sleep. Rattler felt it was time to do the same since he had to be up early in the morning for the mishap board; however, he couldn't shake that email. For now, it, along with Sandy's email, would have to wait.

CHAPTER 16

Rattler stood outside the office in his service dress blue uniform at parade rest, occasionally fidgeting with a uniform that he was not used to wearing. While everyone had told him that he'd saved aircraft 600 and its crew after being hit by the missile, he wasn't feeling very sure of himself right now. If the mishap board deemed he had done something wrong, this could be the end of his career. Time passed slowly for Rattler as people from the ship kept walking by, eyeing him up and down. Life on an aircraft carrier usually never stops, but THE pilot from the famed Hawkeye wearing his dress blue uniform and waiting in the passageway was gaining a lot of attention.

Rattler just wanted this to all be over. He had worked so hard to get to this point in his career, and the thought that it could all be for nothing was getting hard to handle. He remembered what Clipper had said the previous night about being strong and showing confidence, but with each passing minute, that was getting harder and harder. He finally let his mind drift back to his childhood and a memory from Pop Warner football.

"Sorry, but your kid is too big. He'll crush the other kids," the coach said to Rattler's dad.

"How much time does he have and how much weight does he have to lose?" Rattler's dad asked.

"Three weeks and twenty pounds, but maybe this just isn't for him. Have you considered that?" the coach replied.

"See you in three weeks," Rattler's dad promised.

For the next three weeks, a young Rattler ran and ran and ran everywhere he had to go. It was hot, but for extra effectiveness, he would wear a plastic bag under his sweatshirt and sweatpants. He lived a life of complete exhaustion. He consumed very little food and nothing but water to drink, but after only a few days, he started to notice a difference. That alone was enough to drive him on, but as the first week and a half went by, it got tough. His father was always there, encouraging him in his own way. Oftentimes at night, when Rattler was brushing his teeth, his dad would step in with a joke. "You better spit that out!" Every little bit mattered, and as Rattler lost more and more weight, the final weigh-in day loomed ahead.

That morning, he woke up and went running; then he went to the football field. It was signup day, so a lot of people were around—mostly a lot of young children who either looked excited or confused, and a whole lot of fathers ranging from supportive to those reliving their youth through their children. The coach could see the difference in Rattler and suggested to his father that he should run a little more, then go home and take a nap. He was to come back in the afternoon to weigh in but not to eat anything beforehand.

Rattler's father took the suggestion, and as Rattler slid the plastic garbage bag over his shoulders to prepare for yet another run, his father sat down and tightened his own running shoes. He gave Rattler one look and said, "Let's go!" and started running around the track. At first, Rattler was taken back because he'd never seen his father exercise. He was a hardworking man who frankly didn't have the time, but as the shock wore off, Rattler took off to catch his father, his heart swelling with pride. After the run, they went home and Rattler showered and took a nap. Later, his father came in to wake him and tell him it was time. Rattler was nervous.

Sitting on the edge of his bed, his father said, "Listen, you have done the work. You have shown your mother and me, but more importantly yourself, how far you are willing to go. What you have gained from this experience will last far longer than football ever will. Let's get going, but I want you to remember this: no matter what the number on the scale says today, you hold your head up high. Never let them see you break down. Do not give them that satisfaction."

Within an hour, Rattler was at the field house, standing in his boxer shorts in front of a scale with his dad to his left and the team coaches to his right. He looked over at his father who, with a wink and nod, stood a little taller to remind Rattler of what he had said. Rattler took one step and then another onto the scale and opened his eyes…One pound under the weight!

"ENTER!" barked someone on the other side of the door.

Rattler was immediately back on the ship, in the present day, his mind returning to all that had happened over the last few days. He briefly closed his eyes, remembered what his father told him, took a deep breath, and stood tall. *They will not see me break down.* Rattler stepped forward and opened the door.

The room was stark, furnished only with a table and three chairs. Each chair was occupied by a senior officer of the board, none of whom Rattler recognized, but it was clear that the most senior member of the board sat in the center. A US Navy captain with killer eyes trained on Rattler seemed to test his resolve the moment he stepped in. With no other chairs provided, Rattler immediately realized that he was expected to stand. He stepped to a spot marked on the floor, stopped, stood at attention, and checked in.

"LT Jack Owen, reporting as ordered, sir," Rattler said.

"Stand easy," replied the captain across from him. Rattler didn't budge…he would never show weakness.

The next hour went by in a blur as Rattler recounted the events of the night in question from pre-mission planning to the briefing. Once that was complete, and the members of the mishap board seemed content, they went on to question Rattler about the aircraft man-up and launch onto station. By this point, Rattler's nerves were shot, and he wasn't sure how much more of this he could take. But his dad's words kept echoing in his mind, giving him strength. *Never let them see you down.*

The board moved on to questions about what had happened once the missile was airborne, and the questioning seemed to pick up a little bit. Before he knew it, they seemed to be wrapping up. He wanted to talk more and explain more in detail what they went through in the Hawkeye, but then it dawned on Rattler that they already knew all that information from the interviews and pre-mishap work they had done. The captain seemed to sit up a little taller as he concluded. "Listen, son—the bottom line is that what you experienced that night is a first for the Hawkeye community, but that doesn't mean everything was done perfectly and there isn't fault here. Our job is to figure out what went wrong and how to prevent it in the future. You got lucky up there to be able to get that plane back on the ship without loss of life. I cannot tell you what the board findings are, but I can tell you one thing for sure: your career is definitely on a different path now than it was a week ago. Additionally, I have to tell you that you are grounded until further notice. You will not perform any additional duties on board the ship, including standing any type of watch or acting as an LSO. Once our findings are published, you will know our final recommendations and can go forward from there. DISMISSED!"

Rattler turned to the door, exiting without a word. The intensity of what had happened hit him on the other side: no flying or waving as an LSO, just sitting and waiting. He needed to get out of his service dress blues and back into a flight suit. As he walked through ready room two on the way to his room, he noticed that his name had already been taken off the flight schedule for that night and had been moved to the nonoperational side of the board. He was effectively in the penalty box, and it felt weird. Sickboy was there, trying to cover the flight schedule and write up the next day's taskings as well.

"Hey, man—you doing OK?" Sickboy asked.

"Long day; I need a break. Sorry I messed up your schedule," Rattler replied.

"It's OK…I'll figure this out. It's just that we're out of pilots now. With the op tempo we're flying, I have no reserve pilots left if someone gets sick or something. Maybe I can ask one of the CAG staff pilots to fly, but you know how busy they are," Sickboy said as he turned back to his computer.

With that, Rattler decided he was going to go take a nap. There was nothing else to do, and everyone was busy. He left ready room two and went to his stateroom. He got out of his uniform, hanging it back in the closet; he hoped not to need it again for a long time. As Rattler crawled into bed, his mind was racing, but he knew that he needed rest. There was so much going on, and he was just trying to process it all. And then, it hit him: he recalled last night's email—the one to do with the mishap board. Something was up, and there was definitely more to this inquiry than it would appear. Rattler took a few deep breaths to calm down and soon drifted off to sleep.

Chapter 17

After what felt like a full night's sleep, Rattler woke with a start. In reality, he'd only been asleep for a few hours, but it was time to get up and get some food. He was the only one in the room, which made sense since all of his roommates were likely flying or mission planning. After lacing up his flight boots, he checked to make sure he had his room key and cross in his pocket before leaving. The short walk to the ready room was no different than any other time, but as he opened the front door, the back door burst open and Spike came rushing through.

"Two Hornets just had a midair!" Spike yelled to anyone within earshot.

What? So many questions raced through Rattler's mind. *Who were the pilots? Did they eject, or were they still flying? Where were they going?* Rattler quickly realized that he was of zero use to the situation. When that reality hit, Rattler felt totally useless, and anyone who knew him would have said that he looked like a scolded puppy dog. He walked over to the ready room duty desk to speak to one of the squadron maintenance officers, LTJG Andrew "Gunz" Gunner.

"Anything I can help with?" Rattler asked as he looked over Gunz's shoulder to see who was flying.

"I don't know, man, I'm new to this. We have 600 in the hangar for long-term maintenance, and she isn't going anywhere. 602 is coming back to the ship right now on this recovery but doesn't have any fuel to stay airborne any longer." Gunz was doing his best to process the situation.

"What about 603?" Rattler asked.

"They're airborne right now with the CO in the back, but their radar is completely broken, and they are reporting multiple radio failures," Gunz replied.

Rattler took a moment to think. The CO of the squadron, who literally lived for being an E-2C NFO, was in the back of a Hawkeye during a critical time when he could finally make a difference (and more importantly, a name for himself that would likely boost his career), and he didn't have the ability to help at all. For a brief moment, Rattler half smiled, thinking that Karma was a bitch.

"So that leaves 601. What is her status?" Rattler asked.

At that moment, Clipper came through the ready room door like a man with a purpose. Clipper was an interesting guy because he could be the most laid back, relaxed person you've ever met. Tell the guy he couldn't fly for any amount of time, and his first thought would be about how he was going to enjoy the time off and the vacation. On the other hand, when shit hit the fan, Clipper became laser focused to a level that those around him would rise up and also perform at their peaks. He was the most unlikely leader if you really didn't know him, but Rattler was always happy to have him in his corner.

"Maintenance says 601 is fully mission ready; we just need to find a crew," Clipper said, helping Gunz out since he was clearly over his head on this one. "Gunz, call CAG Ops and tell them we can be airborne in thirty minutes. See if they approve it."

"Copy, but who is going to fly it? I am looking for crews, and between people flying, other duties, being sick, etc. I can't find anyone else except for you, and Spike to run the systems in the back," Gunz said.

"Spike, can you handle this alone?" Clipper asked.

"Well, I mean I'm good, but I could use at least one more person back there," Spike replied.

"What about 'Repeat'? Where is he?" Clipper asked.

"He flew earlier and is sleeping in our room right now," Spike replied.

"Gunz, we'll watch the desk here. Run down to the room and see if Repeat feels up to going," Clipper directed.

"Copy; I'm on it," Gunz said, hanging up the phone. "CAG ops approved the launch, and by the way, I heard CAG in the background ordering you airborne in fifteen minutes!"

Rattler stood there for a moment, watching his roommates and friends really step up to the challenge. It was interesting to see in real time because for the longest time, they'd all been just flight students. Whether sitting in the front or the back of the Hawkeye, everyone went through a two- to three-year process of training before joining a fleet squadron where the next training event was the main focus. Generally, there were no other responsibilities besides studying and being ready. Now, just a short time after completing training, this group of junior officers was being thrust into a life-and-death situation—and they were doing great. While Rattler was sad that he really couldn't help, he was also very proud of the fact that his friends were stepping up.

"What are we, are we, are we doing, boys?" LT Ryan "Repeat" Reynolds said as he came through the ready room door. Repeat was one of the best controllers in the squadron. He'd received his call sign because he had a stutter—a condition that immediately disappeared when he was talking on the radio or controlling aircraft. It was actually unbelievable to hear the transformation, and Rattler knew that Clipper was lucky to have both Repeat and Spike in the back of his plane on this night.

"Here's the plan," Clipper explained. "Spike and Repeat, get your asses up to the plane now and make sure we are ready to go. I'm going to finish getting some pre-flight planning crap together and will follow you up there. She's parked on catapult two, and maintenance says she's ready to go, but make sure you look over everything to be sure. No cutting corners tonight, but CAG wants us airborne in fifteen minutes, so get moving! I'll try to find another pilot to go with me, but if I can't, I'll go it alone," Clipper said. With that, Spike and Repeat headed out to get their flight gear on and check out the plane. The ready room was empty now except for Clipper, Rattler, and Gunz.

"Clipper, man, I'm not sure that I can approve you to fly alone," Gunz said.

"Well, frankly, I'm not asking. But if you can find me another pilot who can be ready in fifteen minutes, I'm all ears. We have two Hornets airborne right now who need our help. I get the rules, but I'm the one signing for the plane, so your conscience is clear on this one. I can handle it," Clipper said.

Gunz walked out of the ready room to check with maintenance control about the status of everything while Rattler couldn't help but be annoyed with the situation. Just a few nights ago, he'd flown the shit out of a broken Hawkeye that had been damaged by a SAM, and now he was sitting on the sidelines when people really needed him. He was fed up with the squadron leadership, fed up with his soon to be ex-wife, and really fed up with how this whole deployment was progressing.

Rattler had wanted to be a navy pilot for what seemed like forever, and now he was being prevented from doing just that. His great uncle used to talk about life-defining moments during his career. He'd been a backseater in dive bombers in WWII and would tell Rattler stories of "gut moments" where he'd had to decide to listen to his gut or his brain. He told Rattler that a man who listens to his gut will have a much more fulfilling life. He would always finish up by saying that even if it was difficult to listen to your gut in the moment, your choice was to "get busy living or get busy dying." Those words struck Rattler hard at this moment.

"I'll fly with you," Rattler said quietly to Clipper.

"You can't, bro-dingo—the mishap board and all that. They specifically told you that you were grounded until further notice," Clipper said back.

"Look, here's the deal, man. Name one other pilot you'd rather have up there… That's what I thought. Since you can't do that, here's how it's going to go down. You run up to the plane and I'll finish up around here. I'll meet you up there, but I'm flying in the left seat. Frankly, you have been more involved in talking to people so you can run the mission with Spike while you sit in the right seat. Plus, if I'm hanging my career on the line, I might as well get one last flight, right?" Rattler replied.

"But bro, you are grounded," Clipper repeated with a smirk.

"Dude, we are on a ship surrounded by miles of water. I don't see any ground around here!" Rattler said, laughing.

"Well, shit. Let's get to it, brother," Clipper said as they walked out of the ready room. "I was wondering how long it was going to take you to volunteer for this. I was starting to think that I was going to have to drag you to the plane."

CHAPTER 18

"Engines are coming online," Rattler said over the ICS as both motors stabilized and the E-2C Hawkeye came to life. According to his watch, it had been seven minutes since CAG's airborne request, and everyone in the plane and on the flight deck were working to get the Hawkeye up and away. All systems were checking out, but chatter was kept to a minimum. The Wallbangers had been on deployment for months together, and all four crew members were close friends and roommates. That type of bond, along with the fact that they were all junior officers and knew how to get shit done when needed, was proving to be a great combination.

"I'm ready to taxi when you are," Clipper said over the ICS.

"Screw it. We are good enough back here, brother. Let's get going," Spike added.

Rattler gave the flight deck chief a thumbs up, and they started unchaining the aircraft from the flight deck. Next, a weight board was shown to Rattler, and he indicated his OK.

"You positive you want to do this?" Clipper asked Rattler.

"Let's do our jobs. I'll worry about my career later," Rattler replied.

"Hey, guys—I know you are busy, but this is what I have. Two Hornets had a midair; both are still airborne. CAG is trying to decide where to send them and might bring them back here. CAG ops just called away the alert 5 and 15 tankers and are trying to get more airborne. Sounds like they are going to try and bring them back to the ship, but both Hornets are pretty beat up. I'll give you more info once we're airborne," Spike advised.

"Thanks, buddy—keep it up. We'll be airborne in a minute," Clipper added.

Rattler followed the flight deck director and was ultimately handed over to the yellow shirt for the very short taxi to catapult two on the bow. Clipper ran through final checklists as both Spike and Repeat finished preparations in the back.

"Ditching hatch is stowed, and we are ready," Spike said, indicating that they had taken out the ditching hatch and stowed it. This was standard procedure in case the plane got a soft catapult and ended up ditching in the water. If the ditching hatch was still in place when the plane hit the water, it would be impossible for them to get it out after the fuselage impacted the water.

"Copy," Clipper replied.

"You up for this one?" Rattler said to Clipper with a smile.

"Just a walk in the park," Clipper replied with a laugh.

One thing both had learned early on in their careers was that successful individuals were able to laugh off stress very quickly. To put everything in perspective, less than fifteen minutes before, none of them were planning on flying; in fact, one person had been asleep, and another was grounded. To be able to compartmentalize tasks and get their heads in the game so quickly was critical to safely doing their jobs.

Now their fellow air wing pilots were relying on the Hawkeye to get airborne and help coordinate multiple tanker aircraft in order to save those two F/A-18C aircraft and their pilots. Everyone involved understood the critical nature of the timing involved: they had to get it right the first time and not make any mistakes. They also realized that their actions could very well determine the fate of those pilots, and also that this mission could change from a command and control to a search and rescue at any moment.

As Rattler sat in the front of the E-2C Hawkeye under a load of mental stress that would cripple most men, he took a deep breath and felt in his flight suit pocket for the cross that his aunt had given him. It sat where it always did, and with that, he knew that he would be OK.

What waited for him when he got back on the ship was unknown, and what lay ahead for his career was even more in limbo. For the time being, he was doing the job he had been trained to do, and he would do it to the best of his ability to ensure that those pilots returned safely tonight.

"Stand by for tension," Rattler communicated over the ICS as he felt the ship catapult force the nose of the aircraft down slightly. He instinctually pushed the throttles to max and did his control wipeout while he looked over the engines.

"I like it. You ready?" he asked Clipper.

"This shit never gets old… Light 'em up, brother!" Clipper replied.

A moment later, Rattler flipped on the external lights switch, signaling to everyone on deck that the Hawkeye was ready to go. The aircraft's wheels were in motion now as everyone did their final checks both inside and outside the Hawkeye. If something went wrong on the flight deck, they could suspend the launch, or if the plane's crew saw something they didn't like inside the cabin, Rattler could turn the outside lights off as a signal, but there were no guarantees that they still wouldn't be launched. He'd heard stories of pilots trying to suspend their launch only to get launched anyway. Within seconds, the crew was thrown back into their seats as the Hawkeye accelerated down the catapult and was airborne.

"Better than sex!" Clipper screamed as they became airborne, making their way to a spot in the sky to help coordinate the mission.

Rattler and Clipper fell quickly into their roles while Spike and Repeat, both top-notch NFOs, began setting up the coordination in the back. The NFOs didn't need the aircraft to be in the perfect position to begin their jobs; they could build a mental picture of the airspace and begin preparing to get fuel to the stricken Hornets while also coordinating other tankers to supply the tankers. Once it was all said and done, over twenty airplanes would be on station as they tried to support the Hornets' journey safely back to the carrier.

"Rattler—CAG wants to talk to you on radio three," Spike informed him.

"Seriously?" Rattler replied.

"Yeah, man. Radio three is yours," Spike replied.

"601, this is Barbwire actual. How do you read?" Rattler and Clipper heard after selecting radio three.

The pilots shared a knowing glance as to the identity of the caller. "Barbwire" was the call sign of the air wing, so "Barbwire actual" was CAG himself. Knowing "Nails" as Rattler and Clipper did, they knew he was no-nonsense and wouldn't want to be kept waiting.

"Barbwire, this is 601. Go ahead, sir," Rattler replied, figuring the worst in his head. He assumed that CAG would recall the Hawkeye to the ship since Rattler wasn't supposed to be flying. Ultimately, that meant the end of his career.

"Rattler, is that you?" CAG asked.

"Yes, sir!" Rattler replied, trying to sound confident.

"Ok, son…here's the deal: I need you to tell me exactly how long you can keep that plane airborne tonight. You guys are the only shot at this working, and I need to know the timeline. One look at the ball, no wave off or bolter—understood?" CAG said.

"Sir, we will work a fuel plan immediately and get back to you. Just to be clear, do you want us on the ball with our minimum fuel?" Rattler asked. He was referring to the squadron minimum fuel state for returning to the ship. Every aircraft in the air wing had a minimum fuel; the only difference here was that the other planes could midair refuel, but not the Hawkeye. Essentially, once the Hawkeye's reserves got below 2,500 pounds of fuel, the barricade would be rigged on the flight deck instead of a normal trap. Rattler and Clipper had heard old sea stories of a Hawkeye being barricaded, but no one could confirm if it had actually happened. Landing with 2,500 pounds of fuel aboard would render their weight about 2,000 pounds less than usual, making landing even more challenging.

"Son, let me make this crystal fucking clear: there will be one shot at landing that plane tonight, and it will NOT be a barricade! Work your fuel numbers and tell me what time you need to call the ball behind the ship. You need to get this right. There are lives at stake," CAG underscored.

"Yes, sir. Understood. Stand by," Rattler replied.

"Shit, man…" Clipper said. "Are the fuel gauges even that accurate? How low should we go?"

"Didn't they teach us that the fuel gauges could be +/–250 pounds per engine?" Rattler asked.

"Yeah, that sounds about right," Clipper replied.

"OK, how about this: work us a fuel plan to stay airborne and call the ball with 1,000 pounds total fuel. That could mean we have between 500 to 1500 pounds of fuel for landing depending on the fuel gauge accuracy. Either way, it will give me enough time to land the plane. If I bolter or get waved off, then I will get the plane level, and we all bail out—or at least you three can," Rattler said.

"Well, shit—I never even thought I'd live *this* long… Let's do it," Clipper said.

"OK, give me an airborne time to give CAG," Rattler replied. "Hey, guys! I need you both on ICS for a minute to go over this."

"We're up," Spike said.

Rattler went about laying out the plan to his buddies in the back, giving them the pros and cons and the safety risks involved. He made it very clear that what they were planning was not standard and could get them all in trouble, but that he would take the heat. With zero hesitation, Spike and Repeat agreed to Rattler's plan. They had the utmost confidence in him.

"Barbwire, 601—" Rattler called on radio three.

"601, this is Barbwire actual. Go ahead," CAG replied.

"Sir, we need to be on deck by 1900 Zulu," Rattler replied.

"Copy; expect that," CAG replied.

"Sir, just to be clear, we will have 1,000 pounds of fuel on the ball," Rattler said.

"Copy that, son; expect that. Conserve as much fuel as you can, and plan on that timing. We will be in touch soon," CAG replied.

"Yes, sir," Rattler replied.

"And, son…I'm counting on you and your crew tonight," CAG said.

Soberly, Rattler replied: "We won't let you down."

Based on Clipper's fuel planning, Rattler had already pulled the fuel flow back to optimal. As he deselected the radio, he glanced at Clipper who was busy listening to multiple radios, trying to help Spike and Repeat by keeping track of all the airborne aircraft. There are times while flying that the tempo of time seems to change, whether it speeds up to hone your complete attention or slows down to allow you to take everything in and process it. At this moment, high above the ocean with a minimal crew of junior officers and friends plus a fuel plan that would have him fly the plane far lighter and lower on fuel than he had ever experienced, Rattler was absorbing the immense pressure. There were lives at stake, but there wasn't much he could do except fly the plane the best he could, and hours from now, prepare to land on the first try.

Just then, Spike got on the ICS. "Shit! Aircraft 301 just lost a motor on top of his flight control malfunction. He may have to eject!"

CHAPTER 19

After listening to the controlling radio that Spike was monitoring, Rattler could tell that aircraft 301 was only fifteen miles from the ship; it had been able to refuel but was experiencing flight control problems. Rattler surmised that while tanking, the pilot's nerves were rattled, and he had broken the basket off the refueling aircraft. Worse still, the basket had fallen into the Hornet's number two engine. Nevertheless, the plan was still to try and recover the struggling aircraft aboard the ship.

Rattler immediately knew that this turn of events would cause even more problems. First, that tanker was now out of commission and could not supply any more gas. Aboard the *Nimitz*, crews were already working on recovering it and getting it out of the way. Second, while 301's pilot already had his hands full dealing with the midair and flight control problems, now he was also single engine: this would make landing on the ship much more difficult. Additionally, he was also not able to take on fuel anymore, so whatever fuel he had onboard was it. If the pilot couldn't get the Hornet on deck, he would be forced to fly alongside the ship and eject.

According to his watch, Rattler and aircraft 601 had been airborne for over four hours now. Time seemed to be going by at an accelerated pace, and all Rattler could do from the cockpit of the Hawkeye was to provide backup to Spike and Repeat. He tried not to think too much about who the two Hornet pilots might be—that was enough to keep him from constantly looking at the Hawkeye's fuel gauge, which seemed to be losing fuel faster than normal. In reality, they were burning fuel exactly as planned. Switching over to the radio that Repeat was working on, Rattler could tell that the other Hornet had diverted to a land-based air force base, although he couldn't tell which one. That seemed to him to be a much longer flight, but hopefully a landing there would be more forgiving than one on the ship at night.

Rattler and Clipper had a list of all the aircraft currently airborne, and Clipper was checking them off as they landed. At the beginning of the mission, multiple F/A-18 E/F Super Hornet tanker aircraft had been launched from the ship; some had three drop tanks, and others had five. Once airborne, the tankers had strung out in line astern formation, heading toward the two disabled aircraft. One plane would "tank" or refuel another until they hit the "bingo" fuel, which meant back to the ship. In the meantime, more aircraft were being prepped on the flight deck to keep the process going. The sheer coordination of effort required was immense, but it also made Rattler proud to be part of the team. Everyone from CAG down to the maintenance guys and girls on deck were working nonstop to help those two pilots.

"301 is on final on radio two, guys," Spike said.

Clipper immediately selected that radio so they could hear it in the cockpit.

"301, Hornet ball, 4.6, single engine, flight control problems," radioed the pilot.

"Roger ball," replied the LSO. "You are on glide slope, a little right for lineup," indicating to the pilot what he needed to do.

"You are on glide slope," said the LSO, getting into a rhythm with the pilot to help him land.

"Sounds like he is doing great," Clipper said.

"Way to fucking jinx him," Rattler replied.

"Going a little low; little power, easy with it," radioed the LSO. "We got you, 301!" radioed the LSO as the aircraft was in the wires and stopped.

Rattler and Clipper could hear the cheers in the background from the flight deck LSOs, happy to have their brother home.

"Nice job, Spike," Rattler said over the ICS.

"Thanks, bro—that was a no shitter. One down, one to go," Spike replied.

"OK, give me a rundown on the other aircraft," Rattler replied.

"Stand by…I have to take the handover from Repeat to see where it's at. He should be on the ground soon," Spike replied.

"Looks like we will have plenty of gas and you won't have to perform your glider carrier landing after all," Clipper said to Rattler.

"Yeah, I hope so. Not something I was really looking forward to. We still have to recover a lot of tankers and that will take time, but this seems to be going as planned," Rattler replied.

Rattler thought for a minute about what was going on aboard the carrier right now. He was sure that the flight deck was chaotic, but he was thinking more about the Wallbanger ready room. By now, the skipper had to know that Rattler had disobeyed a direct order, and he was sure that wouldn't make him happy. Adding fuel to that fire was the fact that Skipper was all about himself—it would drive him nuts that he was not up here, controlling the recovery effort, although Spike and Repeat were doing an amazing job.

Rattler wondered how much worse it would be if he had a different crew. He knew he could always count on Clipper. They had already been through so much that there was no doubt in his mind that Clipper was a lifetime friend who would never let him down. He got to know Spike almost from his first day in the squadron as they had checked in about a week apart; he liked Spike a lot too. He was a family man and much more mature than most of the other junior officers, but he also knew how to have a good time. When alone with Rattler, he would often speak very fondly of his wife and his two daughters, and you could tell he was ready to get home to them. As for Repeat, Rattler had only met him within the last six months but immediately liked him. He had a goofy, yet cool demeanor that Rattler found comforting. It was amazing that despite Repeat developing such a strong stutter, it completely disappeared once he was on the radio. Repeat was going to be an amazing controller, and Rattler was proud that he had stepped up for this flight. He was obviously willing to take the risk to help his air wing brothers.

"You guys up?" Spike asked over the ICS.

"Go," Rattler replied.

"OK, so I have bad news and worse news. The bad news is that Skipper is in another Hawkeye on deck and is trying to get it airborne to take over for us. It sounds like the pilots who just landed from their five-hour mission don't understand why they need to take off again, especially since their Hawkeye doesn't have a working radar. Typical micromanagement from the skipper, I guess," Spike said.

"Fucking idiot," Clipper replied. "And the worse news?"

"So, and I still can't believe this, but we are working with aircraft 305 now. I guess he was the more damaged aircraft and was sent to land at an air force base, but he can't," Spike said.

"What do you mean, he can't?" Rattler asked.

"They won't turn the lights on for him. I guess for security reasons or some other reason, they aren't granting him permission to land, so he's headed back to the ship. More tankers are launching, but I'm not sure if he will even make it out here. I guess his centerline drop tank was damaged and it's causing a lot of drag, but it won't jettison so he's stuck with it. He's burned about double the fuel they usually do, but we are trying to work it. I'll give you more info when I have it," Spike concluded.

"Thanks, man," Rattler replied. "What were you saying about that glider approach?"

"Shit, man. Let me re-run these numbers to make sure I got them right," Clipper said. "Plus, it will keep my mind off of how much of a dipshit Skipper is."

CHAPTER 20

"Master caution light," Clipper said.

"Got it: low fuel light. Looks like the right side for now, but the left won't be far behind. Fuel numbers look like they are matching your plan, so I guess we should have expected this," Rattler said.

"Dude, we still have a long time airborne. I guess this is going to be an idle descent out of altitude right to landing?" Clipper said.

"Yup, just going to be a long time to have to stare at that damn light," Rattler replied as his mind raced through how the rest of this flight would go.

"No problem," Clipper said as he reached up and popped the light out of the console and put it in his pocket. "We have enough on our plate right now and don't need any more distractions."

Rattler couldn't help but laugh at the way Clipper handled things, but his mind went back to the situation at hand. They had one Hornet safe on the carrier and another one heading back to the ship. Their Hawkeye was very low on gas, but on the plus side, everything seemed to be working properly. They had been airborne for a long time and the crew was tired, but adrenaline was helping to keep them alert.

"Spike, can you give us an update when you get a chance?" Clipper said over the ICS.

"Yeah, guys. Sorry, I was just about to call you," Spike replied. "Looks like this is starting to work out. Aircraft 305 is making its way back to the ship and is—hang on—about a hundred miles away right now. He has to fly a little slower because of that centerline tank, but so far, so good; however, the pilot sounds completely exhausted. We are starting to recover some of the tankers. There was talk of barricading 305, but they want to try and trap him first. The plan is to get him on deck after all the tankers land just in case there is damage to the flight deck when he lands, or worse. Once all of that clears up, then we will land. How is our fuel doing?"

"You probably don't want to know," Rattler replied. "But we are still on our fuel ladder, so that's good."

"Copy. Thanks guys, we trust you," Spike said. "Oh, hey Rattler, CAG is on radio two for you."

"Thanks bro," Rattler replied.

Rattler switched up radio two. "Barbwire, this is 601," Rattler said.

"Rattler, CAG here. How are you guys doing?"

"Sir, good for the most part. We have low fuel light on one—sorry, both motors now—but we are still on our fuel ladder so I guess that is to be expected," Rattler replied.

"OK, son. The plan is to land everyone else, 305 last, and then catch you. Coordinate with the ship to be ready to start your approach when 305 is approaching. We will have one shot at this. I know you have no gas to spare so I want the timing to work out," CAG said.

"You got it, sir. Clipper and I are on it," Rattler assured him.

"Oh yeah, and I know you are both LSOs, but don't give me any of that hero angel in white bullshit tonight. Fly that aircraft into the wires on the first try. I don't give a flying shit how it looks…just get aboard," CAG ordered.

"Yes, sir," Rattler replied.

"See you on deck, son," CAG signed off.

"Did he just give you clearance to fly a shitty landing?" Clipper joked.

"Yeah, I guess so," Rattler replied.

"Doesn't he know all of your landings are shitty?" Clipper teased.

"Thanks for the confidence, brother," Rattler replied.

Rattler went back to flying the aircraft and started moving to a position closer to the ship. Listening to the radio, it sounded like all of the Super Hornet tanker aircraft were on deck, leaving only 305 and 601 airborne. Timing-wise, it seemed like the time to get this Hawkeye on approach. With that, Clipper told Spike that they were starting their long descent to the ship from 25,000 feet. That would take some time, and as Rattler clicked off the autopilot and pulled the throttles back to idle, he couldn't help but notice the fuel gauges. They seemed to be bouncing around more now that the fuel was low. Rattler tried to ignore the gauges, but it was impossible. He'd never been in a Hawkeye with this little fuel; once again, all that he could do was keep his eyes moving to the other flight instruments and endeavor to fly the plane perfectly.

"Radio two, bro," Clipper said.

"305, Hornet ball 3.6, flight control problems," the pilot radioed.

"Roger, ball, we have you a little low and on centerline," the LSO radioed back.

Rattler turned the radio down so he could hear the vectors for his approach. He wanted to know when 305 was on deck, but he also had other things to do.

"Little power," Rattler heard the LSO say.

Poor guy, Rattler thought. With all the shit that guy had been through tonight and how tired he was, he had to be operating on overload at this point.

"POWER, POWER, WAVEOFF, WAVEOFF, WAVEOFF!!!!" the LSO screamed, sending chills down Rattler's spine. He immediately checked his fuel gauges.

"Shit!" Rattler said to Clipper as he looked over at him.

"305, we have you. Power back—we've got you, son," the air boss confirmed.

"Holy shit, they caught him," Clipper said. "That must have been scary as shit to get that many wave off calls and still trap. I bet he was headed for the back of the ship. Now it's our turn, buddy."

On their descent to the ship, Rattler made sure all the checklists were done, and he briefed his crew on what the plan was. Rattler would fly the plane to the best of his ability and if they got waved off or boltered, then he would level the plane and prepare for bailout. The order out the door would be: Repeat, Spike, Clipper, and then Rattler (after he knew everyone else had gone). Rattler would hold the plane level to ensure his crew had the best chance of survival. If, at any time on the approach, they had engine issues due to fuel starvation, Rattler would discontinue the approach, level off, and issue the bail out order.

"You ready for this?" Clipper asked.

"Yup," Rattler replied.

"Remember, bro: you are light as shit. Keep that power back because it will be easy to bolter, Clipper added.

"Copy," Rattler said. His mind was 100-percent focused on flying the perfect approach in order to make the landing as easy as possible. He was in uncharted waters at this point because he'd never been taught how to fly a plane that was so light on fuel. The Hawkeye was relatively over-powered, so when the plane was this light, it made the landing difficult.

"601, Hawkeye ball 1.1," Clipper said over the radio.

"Roger, ball," replied the LSO.

Meatball, lineup, AOA; meatball, lineup, AOA...was all Rattler could think about now. Going back to his training, he kept his eyes moving from the lens on the ship to his lineup on centerline to the AOA indicator as quickly as he could. He knew it was the only way to notice small deviations that could cause a problem with landing. Approaching the "burble" behind the ship—the area where wind would wrap around the aircraft carrier's tower and cause disruption to the aircraft—Rattler pulled the throttles back and hit the idle stops. He wanted less power on the aircraft but was as far back as he could get.

"Easy with it," the LSO advised.

Rattler started "wagging" the wings and kicking just a little rudder back and forth to try and kill any lift the aircraft was experiencing and stop the meatball from rising. It was a trick he'd learned a long time ago, and it was working now as the ball stabilized and the Hawkeye slammed into the flight deck, catching a wire and coming to a stop.

"Fucking 3 wire!" Clipper said. "Shit hot!"

Immediately after stopping, Rattler released the brakes and felt the wire tug the aircraft back. He could then retract the hook and taxi out of the landing area. Clipper got the wings folded and everyone relaxed: everyone except Rattler, that is. He looked down at the fuel gauges and saw that the left motor was reading 250 pounds, and the right motor was reading 500 pounds. As they turned to the left to line up for the parking spot, the left motor shut down. It was out of fuel.

"Well, I guess we stayed airborne as long as we could, right?" Clipper joked.

They stopped the aircraft and shut down the other motor after being chained to the flight deck. The adrenaline was wearing off quickly, and Rattler wanted to get downstairs and relax. After all the shutdown checks were done and they'd collected everything, Rattler turned to Clipper.

"Thanks, man—couldn't have done it without you," Rattler said.

"Anytime. Nice job, brother," Clipper replied. Someone caught their eye coming into the plane.

"I want your fucking wings right now!" the skipper yelled. "This is bullshit, and I don't want to hear a word from you. Just give me your wings off your flight suit. You are done, shithead. Your navy flying career flying is over!"

Clipper stood up quickly, blocking the skipper from coming into the cockpit. Intimidated, the skipper took a step back. "Get the fuck off our aircraft…sir!" Clipper yelled.

Chapter 21

Rattler's head ached, and he rolled over in his bed. After the exhausting night he'd had, he expected that he would sleep soundly, but he'd been restless and now had a massive headache. At times, he'd woken up thinking that everything was just a dream, but then reality would hit before he tried to sleep some more. He wasn't sure what time it was, and honestly, he didn't care. After he and Clipper got out of the plane the previous night, he went immediately to his room, trying to avoid everything. He was not looking forward to hearing the results of the mishap board, or hearing more from his skipper, who seemed set on ending his career. Additionally, even if the mishap board voted in his favor, he'd still disobeyed a direct order by going flying, and he was sure that decision wasn't going to end well for him. As he lay in his bed, he tried to close his eyes and just relax.

His mind drifted back to days before this crazy deployment. When he'd left home, his relationship with Jennifer had seemed pretty normal and healthy. They had talked about having children, but thought it better to wait until he got back from this deployment. At the time, Rattler was ready, but Jennifer seemed hesitant. She said it was because she wanted him at home, but he was starting to think there was more going on. He always worried that he wouldn't make it through the deployment and that he would never have the chance to be a father or pass on the family name.

All of that seemed stupid now. He'd been shot at, almost run a plane out of fuel, and the squadron leadership seemed hell-bent on railroading his career. The worst part about the whole thing was that Rattler didn't exactly know why. Back in Point Mugu, California, Rattler had worked very hard to become the "go to" guy in the squadron. He would fly when others didn't want to, took ground jobs others didn't want, and generally just tried to help out. He thought of the squadron as his extended family (although lately, it seemed like his only family). Still, he wanted to be a leader.

Rattler's thoughts drifted to the two strange emails he had received a couple of nights before. The one from Jennifer had made it seem like she was almost excited that Rattler had been shot at, or maybe it had something to do with how people were treating the news back on base. Either way, it seemed stupid: Rattler hadn't changed, but maybe now he was something different in her eyes—maybe more of a man, for some reason. Briefly, he thought about how he could try to work it out with her, but then thoughts of the good times were crushed by feelings of betrayal, and he vowed that he was done with her. He had offered before to try anything and everything to make it work, but he wasn't going to beg now; that chapter of his life was over. He opened his phone and realized that in one week, he would be officially single for the first time in his life since college. He expected that realization to be scary but found it a relief. *Close that door and others will open.*

His mind went to the second email. Maybe he had just been overtired when he read it, or maybe that email had never been there in the first place. He'd never had an email just disappear from his inbox, or deleted messages without a trace. It was very bizarre, and he couldn't get the message out of his head. "There is more to things than what appears on the surface. A/C 600's fate is much more than meets the eye." Assuming that the email was real and that he wasn't losing his mind, what did it mean?

Throughout all of Rattler's training on the Hawkeye, he'd never heard of an E-2C getting shot at. He guessed that it was possible, but why wouldn't that have been covered during training? Also, if it had happened in the past, maybe they would have equipped the plane with countermeasures to defeat a missile. The more Rattler thought about it, the more he believed that his mind must have been playing tricks on him. The level of stress on this deployment had just reached a boiling point; he'd been extremely tired that night and had been totally unprepared for the missile ordeal. Just as the body tried to protect itself in times of extreme stress or danger, he was sure that his mind was trying to do the same with the manifestation of that email.

Rattler figured that it was time to get up and start his day. He couldn't lay in his bed forever; eventually, he would have to face everyone. As he crawled out of bed, feeling immense fatigue, he realized he was alone. The curtains on his roommates' beds were pulled back, and one of the lights over the sink was on. He was surprised that he hadn't heard any of them get up: maybe he'd slept harder than he thought.

*Fly, eat, sleep, repeat…*such was the normal routine onboard an aircraft carrier on deployment. As Rattler walked past the lockers on his way to the sink to shave, something on the floor near the door caught his eye. At first, he figured it was just garbage left behind by Ratbreath. He was notorious for being the messy roommate—a habit that drove Rattler crazy. He reached down to pick up the paper and was about to throw it away when he noticed that it was addressed to him. Inside, written in clear block letters, he found: "Keep your eyes open, watch your back. There is more going on than meets the eye."

Rattler's knees felt weak and almost gave out. He wheeled around to double-check that he was alone as his mind began to flood with questions. This message was proof that the email was real! Rattler felt lightheaded, and the room began to spin. Just then, he heard the lock on the door being turned. Rattler assumed a defensive posture: he had no idea what was going on, but he wasn't about to be caught off guard. He quickly looked around for a weapon but found none. He would not go down without a fight.

Clipper's friendly face emerged from a crack in the door. "What's up, man? You look like you've seen a ghost."

"Huh? What? Um, sorry man… I think I'm still tired," Rattler replied.

"Well, all things considered, I doubt that you got a good sleep," Clipper said. "I just came down to see if you wanted to grab some food."

"Yeah, let's go!" Rattler replied, shoving the letter into his pocket.

"What's that?" Clipper asked. "It better not be another stupid email from your ex. One week to go, right? Final countdown!"

"No, it's nothing," Rattler assured him. They headed out of the room.

Chapter 22

Rattler and Clipper had a meal in the forward wardroom, and Rattler couldn't help but notice that everything seemed so normal; it was almost like the previous night's events hadn't happened. He wasn't expecting to be touted as a hero or anything, but he did expect to hear more talk about it. News travels fast on a carrier on deployment, but it just seemed like another day on the *Nimitz*. He got up to grab a cup of coffee, hoping that it would clear his foggy mind. As he walked back to the table, he had to keep reminding himself that this wasn't one very long, intense dream. Clipper could tell that his friend was lost in thought.

"Crazy shit last night, right?" Clipper said with a laugh as he got up to leave. "See you later, bro."

Rattler had no idea what his fate would be with the mishap board, and he figured that at any minute, his skipper would come to tell him that he was off the deployment and never going to fly again. The emotional roller coaster was killing him, but everyone else on the ship seemed to be going about business as usual. He decided that he should check his email again. The ready room wasn't busy; he easily found a computer, sat down, and logged in to find eight emails in his inbox. He immediately scanned for any that seemed suspect, but there was nothing out of the ordinary—just some work emails, one more from Jennifer, and one from his parents. He made his way through his work emails quickly and decided to delete the one from Jennifer without even opening it.

Clicking on the email from his parents, he read about how they were doing back home. Word of the mishap had reached the States, and while they were concerned, they understood that no news was good news. Immediately, Rattler felt like the worst person in the world because in all the craziness of the past few days, he hadn't updated his parents. He thought about how his mom was probably going crazy, checking her email constantly, and how his father was probably trying to put on a tough face, even though inside, he was also really scared and worried.

Rattler hit "reply" and began to write a cryptic email back to them. They had all the code words that he'd given them before deployment to ensure that his emails would make sense. He explained to them that he was safe, and that while a lot of things had happened, he was OK and looking forward to being home and relaxing soon. The ship would soon be pulling into Pearl Harbor to off-load supplies and begin a "tiger cruise" home. (The tiger cruise was an opportunity for members of the *Nimitz* to bring family and friends onboard for the last leg into San Diego.)

While Rattler briefly thought about bringing his parents out for the cruise, he decided against it. He knew they would really enjoy it, but with everything going on, he didn't need the extra stress. Also, he was still trying to decide if he was going to head home early from Hawaii and get things squared away as the newest, single member of the Wallbangers before the rest of the squadron flew home. As Rattler was finishing up his letter, he noticed one more email in his inbox. He hit "send" on the note to his parents before scrolling to the new message. As if disarming a bomb, Rattler cautiously opened the link, but he immediately relaxed when he saw it was from Sandy. A smile crept across his face as he read it.

"Hey, stud—I hope you are hanging in there on that ship full of men without getting your daily dose of down under. I have been flying a lot and trying to save up money so I can take some time off when you get home from deployment, if you would like that. No matter where I am in the world or what I'm doing, the thought of you always makes me smile. I was flying to Dubai the other day with Cheri, and we were laughing about how much fun we had together. I could tell immediately that her feelings for Clipper are different than mine for you. They are definitely all about their physical fun (not that we aren't), but I would suspect that those two would be perfectly happy just humping like bunnies and leaving it at that. I definitely look forward to you showing me around California, if you are still up for that when you get home. There had been some news lately of something happening to a plane like the one you fly, I think. I doubt it was you, but whenever I see news about it on the television it immediately brings me back to our rooftop talk. Looking forward to hearing from you soon, Sandy."

Sandy's message put Rattler's emotional roller coaster on an upswing. His thoughts went back to the time they'd spent together and how much different Sandy was than Jennifer. *Sandy's going to lose it when she finds out that I was the one flying the plane she heard about on the news.* He liked her energy and was looking forward to spending some time with her after this crazy deployment. He vowed to write her back later, but he also needed to get out of the ready room and walk around the ship. Rumor had it that the two Hornets involved in the midair were in the hangar bay. Rattler logged off and figured he would go for a walk down there. It was funny how busy a person could be on an aircraft carrier, but if they clipped your wings and didn't allow you to fly, how boring life aboard became.

CHAPTER 23

Rattler had always thought that the F/A-18C Hornet was a beautiful machine. Designed to be fast and sleek, yet also strong enough to withstand carrier life, the salt air and hard landings after pulling constant G-forces was hard on the Hornet; nevertheless, she was a beauty. It almost hurt to see aircrafts 301 and 305 just sitting there; both aircraft had been relegated to the hangar bay of the USS *Nimitz*, roped off in the corner as if they were in trouble.

The once-sleek lines of both jets now showed considerable damage, causing Rattler to love the plane more. The fact that they could sustain such damage and still land on the ship was amazing to him. While there would be a lengthy investigation, it was pretty clear to Rattler what had happened as he viewed the jets side by side: the two aircraft had been on a collision course, and 305 happened to climb at the last second to minimize the damage.

On 301, the tops of both vertical stabilizers were gone—it almost looked like a giant had come along and just sheared the tops of the tails off clean. Additionally, the refueling probe was still out, but the tip was gone. Walking around the aircraft the best he could, Rattler could see a lot of damage to the right motor, and visible damage (likely from the flames) when the engine essentially ate itself after ingesting the refueling tip and basket. To him, 301's struts looked like they had taken a hard landing since the jet sat slightly canted to one side. Between the two planes, 301 looked to be in better shape. He walked over to 305, and it was clear that the centerline tank had impacted 301's tail. The tank was canted to the side, and if you looked hard enough, it appeared that the whole fuselage was twisted. Aircraft 305 also sat canted to one side. Rattler imagined that its landing was pretty rough too.

Flying an airplane is all about aerodynamics, and the level of design that went into building and developing one of these aircraft was immense. Rattler thought about the extensive wind tunnel testing, engineering, and research involved in the making of such a machine, only to have it impacted by something with such force that it distorted the whole aircraft. The fact that the damaged Hornets still had enough thrust to keep them flying was amazing, but Rattler couldn't help but think about how hard midair refueling would be, let alone trying to land on the ship.

Shipboard flying was all about getting comfortable with your aircraft. Some called it "strapping on the aircraft." You didn't merely fly in the aircraft but rather became one with the machine. Your body would hear, smell, and feel things that your eyes never even saw. It was like the aircraft was an extension of you. To take that bond and completely disrupt it must have been challenging, to say the least.

Rattler felt bad for aircrafts 301 and 305 sitting there in the hangar bay; he also empathized with the pilots. They had been carrying out a training and upgrade flight and would likely be found at fault for the mishap, although he hoped that wasn't the case. Either way, they were likely not going to be flying anytime soon either. Two more aviators with their wings clipped… Rattler walked away and noticed aircraft 600 sitting at the other end of the hangar bay.

Rattler approached the aircraft, and he felt that immediate connection with her, one that hadn't gone away since their miraculous landing after the missile strike. Maintenance personnel were hard at work patching her up and making things right. News was that a technical expert had been flown out to the ship to survey the damage, and while substantial, they were planning on fixing as much as they could and getting special clearance to fly it to San Diego for more research and further maintenance.

Many of the maintenance personnel recognized Rattler and seemed to stand a little taller: they were very proud that he'd been able to get her back on the ship. Rattler was honestly amazed that it had worked out the way it did. It was a tribute to the engineering and design of the Hawkeye, as well as a lot of luck. If the damage was sustained to critical hydraulic components had been any worse, then he would have lost control of the aircraft. Rattler would not only have been unable to get the aircraft back aboard the ship, but he also wasn't sure that he could have held it level enough to let the crew bail out. It would have been a catastrophic end, so he was happy that the aircraft had held together. As Rattler stood there, studying every aspect of the damaged Hawkeye, he didn't notice the maintenance officer Shotgun walk up.

"Pretty amazing, huh?" Shotgun asked.

"Yeah, I'm still trying to wrap my brain around it," Rattler replied.

"Yeah, I bet. And then last night… Holy crap, man. Are you out for a hat trick or something?" Shotgun joked.

"No, I think my flying days are done. No way Skipper will let me in one of these again," Rattler said.

"Well, that's why I came down here to find you. Skipper wants to talk to you. Listen, before you go, I just want to say that you did it right. I wouldn't have done anything differently than you did and neither would any of the other department heads. We let Skipper know that this morning. I don't know what is going to happen, but I just wanted to let you know that we support what you did, and shit, man—I'm damn proud to be in the same squadron as you," Shotgun said.

"Thanks, and I appreciate that. I doubt it will be enough to deflect the wrath of Skipper, but at least when I am on the C-2 Greyhound (COD) and leaving deployment early, I can hold my head up high," Rattler replied.

"Look, I get it…this sucks. But have faith in yourself. Go see the skipper and hold your head up high. You are a naval aviator, and there is a long tradition that goes back many years behind those wings on your chest. You can't control what the old man is going to do to you, but you can control how you react. Walk in tall, take your beating, and don't show weakness. Guys like him love being able to break down people who intimidate them," Shotgun said.

"Thanks, and copy all," Rattler said, walking off to find the skipper.

Chapter 24

Rattler had gone back to his room briefly to spruce up a bit before trying to locate the skipper. The note on the schedule board said that he was in his stateroom, so Rattler made his way down the long passageways to the skipper's quarters. The skipper didn't have any roommates, so on a positive note, there wouldn't be anyone else to hear Rattler getting his ass chewed out. He knocked on the door.

"Enter!" the skipper called from behind the door.

Rattler walked into the modest room/office that had one bed that converted to a couch, plus a desk and a couple of lockers. Like most other members of the squadron, the skipper had decorated his room with photos of his family to remind him of home. Rattler entered, and the skipper was sitting at his desk, looking over some reports. He barely gave Rattler a glance and went back to what he was doing. Rattler could feel the tension in the room and tried to break the silence.

"You wanted to see me, sir?" Rattler said standing at attention.

"Yes, give me one second," the skipper replied. He went back to reading whatever was in front of him while Rattler took in his surroundings. The life of a squadron skipper obviously wasn't easy. The higher your rank, the greater the number of people under your direction and the fewer peers or friends. Rattler realized that it must be lonely when you make that rank and have that position.

No matter what Rattler had been through, he could always count on Clipper, Spike, Repeat, and to some degree Ratbreath, to be there for him. He was very happy to have them as roommates during this deployment and couldn't imagine how different things would be if he was in some other room. It was the little things that got Rattler through a deployment, or any challenging time, for that matter. If Rattler had to go it alone, he wasn't sure he could make it. The skipper finally finished what he was doing. He closed the file folder and turned to Rattler.

"OK, OK, I'm done. Relax, son; have a seat," the skipper said.

Rattler was immediately taken aback and wasn't sure what angle the skipper was coming from. In the past, he'd always acted so harshly toward Rattler; now he was almost like a different person. Rattler sat in a chair next to the skipper's desk, upright and cautious.

"Look, I want to clear the air and put all of this out on the table. I know a lot has happened in the last week; it is not lost on me that you have disobeyed direct orders multiple times. When I went to the Naval Academy, it was instilled in me that orders are to be followed without question. When you go out on your own, it breeds an atmosphere that undermines everything I am trying to do here," the skipper said.

Rattler could almost feel the setup and was ready for the final blow to his career to come out of the skipper's mouth at any second. "Never let them see you flinch," Rattler remembered his father saying.

"So, with all that being said, we have to see how we can move forward from here," the skipper continued. "That night with the SAM will likely go down in history of the Hawkeye community, and your name will forever be attached to it. It took excellent airmanship to successfully keep flying that plane, let alone bring it back to the ship. While I cannot say that you did it with ease, it is clear to me that you have a skill set that is unique and valuable to the navy. I just finished reading the full mishap report here." The skipper tapped the file on his desk. "I agree with the findings and will be writing my endorsement to be sent to CAG. The bottom line is that you were not at fault. You ultimately saved that aircraft—a national asset—as well as the lives of your crew and who knows how many people on the flight deck. Well done, son."

Rattler sat there, confused. He said nothing and just nodded to the skipper's remarks. Maybe he had the old man all wrong? As Rattler sat there trying to reevaluate the situation, the skipper continued.

"Now, moving on from that, we have to address what you did last night. You were ordered by the mishap board not to fly, nor to engage in any other shipboard or squadron duties. You took it upon yourself and flew anyway. Can you explain yourself?" the skipper asked.

Rattler broke his silence and was now back on the defensive. "Sir, I was keeping to myself all day and just happened to walk into the ready room. The maintenance chief ran in and told us what had happened. Gunz was on duty; he seemed a little overwhelmed being new to sitting SDO, so I tried to help out but was well aware of my orders and tried to keep my distance as much as possible. Clipper and Spike were there helping and putting together a plan. We were short on aircrew, and Repeat volunteered to go, but that left us a pilot short. Clipper was fully prepared to go fly by himself, but I couldn't let him do that so I said I would fly.

"I knew the risks and possible career implications from my decision, but at the time, the lives of those two Hornet pilots outweighed all of that. I made the decision alone. I asked Clipper, Spike, and Repeat if they had any objections to me flying the plane and they did not. We operated according to all squadron operating procedures other than our landing fuel state, as directed by CAG. I take full and sole responsibility for my actions," Rattler concluded.

The skipper sat there, pretending to be thinking something over just for added effect. "OK. Well, obviously I would have preferred to have another pilot fly it so I didn't have to answer to the higher ups as to why my grounded pilot was flying, but on the other hand, you and your crew operated to the highest standard and made the Wallbangers look great, which I appreciate. In fact, I will be putting Spike and Repeat in for awards for their actions last night. CAG was pleased with how you and Clipper handled the plane, and he tells me that landing that low on fuel would be very tricky, so again, you made our squadron look good there too. I have decided that no negative action will come to you or your crew from this because of the favorable outcome.

"I am returning you to full flight duties immediately; you'll likely fly tonight or tomorrow. At the All Officer's Meeting (AOM) tonight, I will be announcing the news CAG told me today, but I might as well tell you now. The ship is heading for a port call after everything that has happened. In two weeks, we will be pulling into Perth, Australia, for just under a week. I have been directed to give maximum time off and CAG told me specifically that you, Clipper, Spike, and Repeat are to have zero squadron duties. That is all I have for you, son. Unless you have any questions, you are dismissed and I will see you at the AOM."

Rattler stood up immediately, still in shock. "Thank you, sir. No questions." Rattler moved to leave; he just wanted to get out of there as quickly as possible.

As Rattler got to the door, the skipper said, "Rattler, clearly I've learned that keeping you on my side and working *for* me is easier than trying to crush you like a little bug. I mean, it's not like I can just have you killed or something, right?" Skipper laughed.

Rattler half smiled and faked a laugh as he walked out the door and shut it behind him. He made his way back to the ready room, but he couldn't get Skipper's last comment out of his mind: it rang eerily of half joke and half truth.

CHAPTER 25

"What the fuck do you mean you two idiots are getting medals and I'm not?" Clipper called out in the room. "I mean, don't get me wrong—you guys rocked up there—but it would have been hard to do all that coordination without the plane being airborne. We never get any credit."

Rattler had gone directly to his room from the skipper's quarters and found Clipper, Spike, and Repeat hanging out. While the skipper never said to keep their meeting confidential, it's widely known that roommates are almost closer than family, so Rattler told his friends what had happened. Of course, Clipper was mostly kidding about the medals because none of them really cared about awards. That isn't why they did the job, or why they'd gone flying that night.

"I love it when you get him worked up," Spike said. "But you said you have more news?"

"Yeah, what's going on?" Clipper asked.

"Well, that's the best part. This is going to come out shortly at the AOM, but whatever. In two weeks, we're pulling into port…in Perth, Australia," Rattler announced.

The room erupted with excitement. Clipper was jumping around and had completely forgotten about not earning an air medal. He couldn't have cared less; he just hoped that he could hook up with Cheri again while they were there. Repeat was just happy at the thought of getting off the ship and having some time to relax. Spike, being a family man 'til the end, was looking forward to spending a lot of time on video chat with his family.

Rattler had honestly thought he'd end up more like Spike in terms of family commitments, but because things hadn't worked out with Jennifer, it looked like that plan was changing. Rattler had to admit that time off the ship would be great. There was a lot going on in his life at the moment, and he needed some time to decompress. He had always prided himself on being able to handle anything, but the pressures had begun to take a toll. The maintenance issues with aircraft, the SAM, the rescue mission where they damn near ran out of fuel… And then to add on that, he was almost a single man; it was all affecting him, and he knew it.

Rattler remembered back to early on in his Hawkeye flight training. The instructor had talked about what it was like to fly a multicrew aircraft around the carrier without ejection seats. It was a serious talk that all Hawkeye pilots hear or think of themselves. As the aircraft commander, it was critical that you took care of the plane and the crew. Rattler knew full on that when he got into the plane, everyone was relying on him to make the right decisions and bring them back in one piece; there were no other options. Maybe this little break would help recharge his batteries and get his edge back.

"How many days in port?" Clipper asked.

"Looks like they are planning six days—just enough to keep us all night current," Rattler replied.

Everything done on the carrier revolved around keeping the pilots' night-landing current. Each pilot needed one night trap every seven nights, or they would fall out of currency. Not a huge deal, but if they went out of currency, they would need to get a day trap before going at night. In the Hornet and Super Hornet squadrons, that wasn't a big deal since a lot of the time their pilots flew twice a day, anyway and their flights were typically a lot shorter than the Hawkeye's. When the Hawkeye took off, it was usually close to five hours before it would land again, sometimes longer. That left little time for the pilot to fly again. The Wallbanger operations department was probably already working hard to figure out how to keep everyone as current as possible in the next two weeks.

"Oh, and CAG has ordered Skipper to ensure that the four of us don't stand any watch in port for our actions last night," Rattler added.

The room erupted again. Even when they pulled into port there was work to be done, so having six days off in a row was unheard of. This could be the reset that everyone needed to get through the rest of deployment and get home with their sanity intact. None of the roommates had ever heard of a port call free from duty, but they weren't about to complain. Rattler wasn't sure how the rest of the officers would feel when required to make up for their absence, but he hoped it wouldn't cause too many problems.

"I guess we need to get to the AOM," Spike said.

"Yeah. Let's…let's…let's pretend like we don't know any of this," Repeat suggested.

Repeat and Spike left the room, and Rattler felt like he needed to tell someone about the final comment the skipper had made to him. Clipper was his closest friend; he needed someone to see if this was all adding up. The email, the letter under the door, and then the skipper's unsettling comment; it just all felt weird.

"Hey man, I have to tell you something Skipper said to me when I was leaving his room," Rattler began.

"Dude man, who gives a shit what he said? You are flying again, we get six beautiful days off in Australia, and you are in the final countdown to officially being a single man. The only thing you need to be thinking about is resting up for all your time with Sandy," Clipper replied. "Now, let's get up to the ready room and get this AOM over with. Shit hot news, brother! I'm stoked!"

CHAPTER 26

The AOM went exactly how Rattler expected it to go with the skipper relaying what he'd already told Rattler. The squadron was very excited to hear about the port call and getting a break. When he mentioned about the four crew members not standing watch in port, the junior officers actually seemed proud to help out. Rattler was impressed with how close-knit the squadron junior officers were becoming. Following the AOM, the junior officers had a meeting to go over a few things, and overall, the new guys were excited to get the admin set up in Perth. Rattler anticipated a good time; he really hoped to get to know Sandy better to see if there was anything between them.

A few days passed, and shipboard life returned to normal. Rattler flew a few times both as aircraft commander and as copilot for new pilots working on getting signed off on their qualifications. He also was an LSO one day that the weather was really bad. While it was a long, hard day, his LSO team worked flawlessly together, and even though the conditions were challenging, nothing major went wrong. Rattler enjoyed being on the LSO platform almost as much as flying. It was an opportunity to challenge himself in a different way and get outside the skin of the ship. He was acquainted with a few surface warfare officers who worked on the nuclear reactor, and they seemed never to see the light of day; Rattler had no idea how they survived a deployment.

A milestone in Rattler's life came and passed with little fanfare. The required "cooling off" period for divorce had passed, and Rattler was officially single again. If not for a short email from Jennifer, and Clipper bringing him an extra piece of cake at dinner with a candle in it to celebrate his "freedom," he would have barely noticed. When he'd learned that Jennifer wanted a divorce, it had shaken his world to the core, but he was getting used to the idea of starting over. He hoped to find someone with whom to share the future.

All that being said, one last thing had to be done, and that's what brought Rattler up to the fantail of the ship late at night, all alone. He found the flight deck to be a very interesting place. During flight operations, it was the most insane and chaotic place to be—injury and potential death were everywhere, if you weren't careful. The noise level was deafening and could also be very disorienting. In contrast, by nighttime, it became insanely quiet. Not much of anything went on, and the stillness was almost eerie. It was hard to see very far if you didn't have a flashlight, and while you still had to be careful, it almost felt like a sanctuary; that's the reason Rattler was up there.

Rattler had worn his wedding ring from the day of his marriage. It symbolized a lot to him, and he was very proud of it. While on board the ship, there were dangers in wearing a ring, so he would clip it to his dog tags and keep it in his flight suit pocket. It was always near him, and as soon as he left the ship, it would go back on. While Rattler stood on the rear flight deck looking over the white wake, he reached into his pocket and found the ring. Unclipping it from his lanyard, he put his dog tags back in his pocket.

He couldn't see the ring very well in the darkness, but he felt it in his hand. Memories of a different life flooded back. From the moment he and Jennifer had been married in a small, base church in Corpus Christi, Texas, to the many moves together, he remembered her fondly. It wasn't until he came back from his first deployment that things seemed to change. She'd met different friends, acted differently, and almost seemed like a completely different person from the girl he met in college.

Over time, it was clear that her goals and even her values were changing, but people didn't stay the same for their whole lives, and Rattler understood that. Once the marriage started to unravel, Rattler did what he thought was best, but he still needed to keep working at the squadron. People relied on him, and he couldn't let them down. While there had been setbacks in his life before, this was the first time Rattler felt as if he'd truly failed at something.

Up on the flight deck of the *Nimitz,* Rattler decided that living in the past wasn't going to get him anywhere, so as the fresh air blew at his back and the salt air stung his nose, he closed his eyes. He said a prayer to his grandfather to look over him going forward and to allow him to be the man he wanted to be. He prayed that his family stayed safe and that Jennifer found what she was looking for. He prayed for the safety of his squadron mates and the other aircrew in the air wing, as well as everyone who was deployed fighting this war, far from home. Chills ran down his spine much like they always did when he talked to his grandfather through prayer. He had fond memories of him from his childhood and believed that he was always there close to him, helping him make the right decisions. He was thankful for that bond.

When his prayer was done, Rattler opened his eyes and looked down in his hand at the simple ring that had once represented everything to him. After running it through his fingers one last time, he reared back and threw it as far as he could into the ocean. With it went all the weight of his past, replaced by optimism for the future. A smile crept across Rattler's face, and he finally felt free.

CHAPTER 27

Perth, Australia, was a beautiful place. Of course, that assessment may have had a lot to do with the fact that the crew hadn't been off the ship since their hurried departure from Dubai. Either way, seeing the city come into view from the ship immediately lifted Rattler's spirits. He had been emailing Sandy over the last few days, trying to make plans. She seemed very eager to get together and was a little upset that she would be away the day the ship pulled into port.

Rattler wasn't too worried about that because of all the free time he was going to get. He didn't tell Sandy that part; he just told her to make plans for things they could do while he was in port. Their initial meeting felt like a lifetime ago, but he really liked Sandy and hoped that his feelings for her were still the same. Only time would tell.

"Cheri is stoked to see me, bro!" Clipper said, walking up behind Rattler on the flight deck.

"Oh yeah?" Rattler replied.

"Yeah. I guess the news of what we did is all over the world, and she thinks I am a real-life hero!"

"How much did you embellish the story?" Rattler asked.

"Not at all," Clipper laughed. "Trying to be real with this one. In the past, I always tried to make things bigger than they were, but with Cheri, it seems like she actually digs who I am."

"Good luck, man," Rattler said as he watched the city get closer.

"Dude, are you bummed that Sandy won't be there tonight?" Clipper asked.

"No man, it's all good. You and Cheri can hang out, and I will stick with the squadron and see what happens," Rattler replied.

"Dude, I told Cheri that night one is for the boys. She wants to stop by, but just because I have a smoking hot flight attendant waiting for me doesn't mean I'm not getting drunk as hell with you first. We have a lot to celebrate. You didn't die when that SAM hit you, we didn't run out of gas, and remember: you are finally fucking single!" Clipper exclaimed.

"That's true, man. Just be yourself with Cheri. You are a great guy, and I'm sure she'll dig you," Rattler assured him.

"If not, that's cool too. I'll just have some fun for six days in port," Clipper said. "Do you have your stuff ready? We are first off the ship."

"Yeah, it's in the room. Let me go down there and grab my bag, and I'll meet you in the hangar bay," Rattler said.

"OK, don't be too long. Spike and Repeat are already down there."

Rattler looked one more time at the city and then headed to his room. He loved the feel of the ship right before a port call, that sense of the ship's energy being renewed. Life at sea, regardless of whether forces were at war, peace, or just training tended to get monotonous. Whenever the crew knew that a port call was coming, it was as if life was brought back to their world. Some dreamt of time away from the ship, while others just wanted to see a new place. Still others looked forward to some much-needed privacy to call home, or just be with their own thoughts. Rattler looked forward to a refresh as well.

It was difficult to walk around the ship right before a port call because everything was happening at once. Some people had duties to attend to before they could leave, others were already packed and ready to go, and some who lagged behind their friends were running around like crazy to just catch up with them. No one wanted to be left behind when it was time to leave.

All the training had been done, and members of the Wallbangers had signed the required documents stating that they understood how to behave in port. Rattler spoke to each member of the division for which he was responsible, listening to that person's plan and relaying his expectations. He also told all his division where he would be staying and how to get a hold of him. He would rather have to come and get them before the skipper found out they were in trouble.

When Rattler got back to his room, he changed into his khaki pants and polo shirt. As an officer, he still needed to look somewhat presentable when coming and going from the ship. Clipper, Spike, and Repeat were already in the hangar bay, and Ratbreath was on SDO watch. Ratbreath had made it clear that he thought it was bull that he had to stand watch on the first day of leave, but that's the way things go.

Before a port call, the junior officers meet and divide up all the watch standing duties that are required. Once they know all the duties, assignments went in seniority order, and people picked what they wanted to do. Since Ratbreath was relatively junior in the squadron, he chose later and ended up with duty on the first night. Everyone took their turn at being junior, so when Ratbreath complained about it to his senior roommates, he didn't receive much sympathy.

As Rattler got his bag from the now empty room, he had to laugh at Ratbreath. He had no doubt that one day he would be a great pilot, senior officer, and LSO, but it was almost like he was trying too hard right now. He just had to do his time, work his way up, and then he would be respected. Respect can't be bought; it takes time to earn. Rattler looked around the room one more time to make sure he hadn't left anything behind, and he saw a white piece of paper being slid under the door. He figured it was just the laundry form, or mess hours for the time in port. When he went to grab it, he saw it was blank except for the words: "Watch your back in port."

Rattler immediately opened the door, stepping into the passageway and looking both ways, but no one was there. Past events flooded his mind: the mysterious email, the first letter under his door, his skipper's unusual comment, and now this. Rattler stepped back into the room and closed the door. He checked that he was actually alone and then stood in front of the sink, looking in the mirror. None of this made any sense. *Why would someone be out to get me?* His mind raced as he tried to remember pissing anyone off while on deployment. Other than the skipper, no names came to mind. All that had changed recently when the skipper seemed to praise Rattler for making the Wallbangers look good in CAG's eyes, which in turn, made the skipper look good too. Lost in his thoughts, Rattler didn't notice the door to his room swinging open.

"Bro, what the hell?" Clipper asked impatiently.

Regaining his composure, Rattler tried to explain. "Sorry, man. I was just grabbing my things and then—"

"Dude, no time. Let's go. I already signed you out in the ready room. Let's get off this ship!" Clipper urged.

"Dude, I've got to talk to you about something important," Rattler insisted.

"It can wait until we get to the hotel, man." Clipper grabbed Rattler's bag and began walking out of the room. "Smile, bro! First port call as a single man!"

CHAPTER 28

Rattler sat at the hotel bar, nursing a beer while thinking about that second note. He was trying to figure it all out while also keeping an eye on his surroundings. Sailors from the ship were making their way ashore, and groups filtered in and out of the hotel lobby; Rattler had to laugh at how easy it was to spot a US Navy sailor in port.

The hotel bar gave him a good view of the front door to the hotel, plus the mirror behind the bar gave him a clear view of anyone approaching from behind. He was starting to feel paranoid: something wasn't right. Between the multiple malfunctions and the SAM incident, the numerous issues were beginning to feel overwhelming. No one else seemed to notice; they all just chalked it up to the inherent risks involved in naval aviation.

As Rattler tried to enjoy his beer, he noticed the skipper walking toward the hotel entrance. He thought it was odd that he was off the ship so early because he always said that officers should be last. He watched the skipper, hoping not to be seen at the bar. Then, Rattler noticed two men approach the skipper, each man appearing to be a carbon copy of the other. Tall, dark-haired and sporting full beards, the strangers were wearing cheap suits with long jackets, which Rattler found odd considering how warm it was. After a brief conversation, they all walked outside, got into a dark-colored SUV with tinted windows, and sped off. Rattler took a look around to see if anyone else had noticed the three, but everyone just seemed to go about their business.

"Bro! I love being off the ship!" Clipper called out as he and Cheri walked up from around the bar. It was apparent from Cheri's hair and Clipper's grin that they had already taken the time to get to know each other again. Cheri looked very happy, and Rattler hoped that Clipper was just being himself and not trying to put on an act for this girl.

"Hi, Rattler," Cheri said. "I'm sorry that Sandy is working tonight, but she is scheduled to be home sometime tomorrow."

"Hey, Cheri. That's OK. I understand how the business is. How have you been?" Rattler replied.

"I've been great—just working a lot and reading some very naughty emails from this guy here," Cheri joked as she punched Clipper's arm. "I'm really happy you guys got to visit Perth. It is just such a great city with so much to see and do. I was upset that I have a trip to go on in a few days, but I think Clipper has convinced me to call in sick. He said I looked under the weather and should spend some time in bed."

"Enough talking; time for shots!" Clipper cheered as he got the bartender's attention and ordered shots for three.

"This first round of shots is for Rattler," Clipper said as he held up his glass. "To the greatest pilot on the *Nimitz* and the newest member of the Wallbangers to be single and ready to mingle. He has saved my life more times that I can count, and there isn't another pilot I would rather fly with. Regardless of what crazy shit this life throws at him, Rattler always finds a way to handle it. No better man!"

"Thanks, man," Rattler said after taking his shot. "I appreciate the words, but is there any way you can peel yourself away from Cheri long enough for us to talk?"

"Dude, I'm not sure a nuclear warhead could separate us," Clipper said.

"It's OK, sweetie, I understand. Let me run upstairs to the room and freshen up. Give me about thirty minutes and meet me up there?" Cheri requested.

"Ok, but if his story is boring, I'm meeting you in the shower!" Clipper replied, laughing as Cheri smiled, kissed him, and walked off. Clipper couldn't take his eyes off Cheri, and for good reason. She was wearing tight black pants, a sleeveless shirt, and high-heeled boots—impressive from any angle.

"Dude, she is a spark plug," Clipper said.

"I can tell that and I'm stoked for you, man, but I have to tell you something," Rattler said, vying for Clipper's attention.

"OK, OK, I'm listening, but you've got thirty minutes. I need more time with her before we get together for dinner and partying tonight," Clipper replied.

"Gotcha. OK, let me run down some things that have happened to me since that SAM hit the Hawkeye," Rattler replied. He went on to tell Clipper about the crazy email that seemed to disappear, which was followed by the first note under their stateroom door. He then discussed the whole conversation in skipper's stateroom, and ended by telling him about the second note slipped under their door earlier today.

"Damn, man… That might be something, but it could also be you looking for something that isn't there. I mean, you have had a lot on your mind lately between all the flying, the divorce, and just being on deployment. Our minds can have ways of playing tricks on us," Clipper said.

"Yeah, I understand that, but there is another thing… Let's go up to my room so I can tell you. I just don't feel safe talking about it here," Rattler said, ordering two more drinks for them.

Rattler and Clipper took the elevator up to the floor where their rooms were located and noticed how much busier the hotel was getting.

"This place is going to be a blast tonight," Clipper said.

"Yeah, for sure," Rattler replied. As they rounded the corner, Rattler noticed that the door to his room was slightly ajar.

"Dude, did you close your door?" Clipper asked, noticing it at the same time.

Rattler's heart sank, and the hair on the back of his neck immediately stood up. Something wasn't right, and he could feel it. The hallway was empty except for the two of them. Rattler approached cautiously and slowly opened the door, trying to ready himself for whatever or whoever was on the other side. The room was very modern and not too big.

Rattler hadn't opted to pay for a suite like Clipper's because he felt that he didn't need to impress Sandy. Hopefully, she would just be happy to see him. He was happy about that decision now because he could view the whole room from the doorway. It was empty; however, it had been ransacked. With Clipper following close behind, he made his way into the bathroom to ensure that it was clear.

"Geez, man…what the hell?" Clipper said.

"See? Something *is* up," Rattler replied as he closed the door. "My mind isn't imagining *this*," he said, motioning around the room. Rattler went on to describe what he'd seen with Skipper this afternoon while he was sitting at the hotel bar. Clipper sat in a chair, trying to piece it all together as Rattler looked through his bag to make sure nothing had been stolen, or placed there.

"Dude, do you have the other two notes?" Clipper asked.

"Yeah, why?" Rattler asked.

"Because, look at this…" Clipper said and held up a note written on hotel stationery. It simply read: "Stop trying to be a hero or you won't make it home."

"Holy crap!" Rattler read the message, and his face turned white. He retrieved the other two notes from his pocket and handed them to Clipper. He laid them all out on the bed.

"The handwriting matches," Clipper said. They both looked over them. "OK, so your mind isn't playing tricks on you, but what the hell does all this mean? You're just doing your job."

"I don't know, man, but I really don't know who to go to with this," Rattler replied.

"No one!" Clipper said, seemingly sobering up by the second. "Something major is going on here; I think the skipper is behind all this."

"Wait, what? I know he said that crap in his stateroom, but do you really think he meant it? The old man just talks nonstop all day, not really meaning anything."

"Remember back to when you had the hydraulic problem in 602?" Clipper asked. "Remember the next morning when I heard Shotgun talking to Skipper and he said that the skipper knew the plane had issues but chose to ignore it?"

"Yeah..." Rattler replied.

"Well, the skipper is constantly talking about how our planes and their systems are lacking, but no one listens to him; he is just another NFO skipper who has something to prove. CAG doesn't like him, and the vibe I get from the other skippers is that they don't like him either. What if he was trying to sabotage our planes to get the navy to put more funding into the squadron? The role of the Hawkeye is an important one, but remember that the skipper grew up thinking that he was going to be searching for Russian bombers and saving the aircraft carrier during his career, not sitting back there listening to planes check in and check out of some airspace."

"Dude, don't you think that is a little far-fetched?" Rattler queried.

"I'm not sure, man. You know me... If you'd come to me a week ago with an email and told me about the conversation with Skipper, I would have said you needed a drink. Add in the notes, and your room looking like this, and I have to agree that something is up. My bet is that Skipper's involved," Clipper said firmly.

"OK, so what do we do now?" Rattler asked.

"First off, don't trust anyone and let's stick together," Clipper said. "Damn it... I was hoping to have some serious alone time with Cheri."

"Dude, let's take a deep breath here," Rattler replied. "We were going to hang out a ton anyway, and we'll always be around other squadron members, so I think we are safe. I think the most important thing is to act normal. If we freak out right now, whoever is doing this will know that we know and something may happen. Let's pretend nothing is going on and keep a low profile. We'll watch over each other like we always do and get to the bottom of this shit. I'll tell you one thing; if Skipper is sabotaging planes for his own agenda, I will kill that son of a bitch!"

A knock on the door startled both of them.

"I'll go check it out," Rattler said.

"OK," Clipper replied, looking around for something he could use as a weapon.

Rattler walked to the door and looked cautiously through the peephole. He saw Cheri on the other side. She looked impatient as she knocked again.

"It's Cheri," Rattler said, opening the door. She burst in and immediately ran to Clipper. She'd clearly been crying and looked very scared.

"What's going on?" Clipper asked.

"I was just finishing in the shower when I heard a knock on the door. I thought it was you and that you'd forgotten your key, so I put on a towel and went to the door. When I opened it, there was a man standing there in a mask. He said, 'Your boyfriend needs to butt out or it will get you all killed.' And then he pushed me and slammed the door shut as he ran off."

Clipper pulled Cheri tight to try and calm her down. He spoke over her shoulder to Rattler: "OK, now I'm involved, and I'm going to kill whoever did this."

CHAPTER 29

Clipper and Rattler waited as Cheri finished getting ready, and then they packed all their belongings. After what happened in Rattler's room, the hotel manager agreed to give them both suites at the adjoining hotel. He wanted to keep the whole incident quiet because of the business that the hotel was getting from the port call. Rattler and Clipper agreed not to say anything; Clipper said that in return, they deserved an upgrade. Rattler was about to object when the hotel manager said that both penthouse suites were open and gave them the keys. *Pretty hard to turn that down*, Rattler thought.

Rattler and Clipper agreed to get set up in their new rooms and then meet up to go to the squadron party together. They had no idea who to trust and didn't want to tip anyone off before they really knew what was going on. After getting to the suite, Rattler began to regret the upgrade. The room, if you could call it that, was massive. It overlooked the city and was actually multiple rooms with a hot tub that sat directly in front of a huge, panoramic window that under normal circumstances would provide an amazing view. The hotel assured them that their identities would be protected, and they had actually booked the rooms under false names.

Rattler was switching between feeling nervous and feeling safe. He knew Sandy would enjoy the room once she got there. Rattler decided to take a shower. After double-checking that the room was locked, he put an empty beer bottle on top of the door handle. It was a trick he remembered from a movie and would alert him if anyone tried to open the door.

The shower, like everything in the room, was massive. It was clearly designed for a party of about ten people, but right now, all Rattler cared about was trying to clear his head. The hot water ran over his head and shoulders as he let the stress melt away so he could concentrate on what was going on. He had a reputation of being able to handle anything thrown at him in the air, and now it was time to do the same on the ground. Looking back at the facts, he had to think about the hydraulic issue on aircraft 602, which he had barely been able to land. Next came the SAM that severely damaged his plane and almost cost that crew their lives. That flight occurred immediately following port call in Dubai, and in conjunction with the Navy SEAL mission. He thought back on the planning for that and while it was rushed, he didn't recall who had set up where the Hawkeye was going to fly that night.

Rattler finished his shower and dried off, still trying to make sense of it all. The mysterious email could be chalked up to anyone who had any IT knowledge on the ship. While Rattler knew how to fly airplanes well, he assumed someone could set up an email that would delete after it was opened. That led him to the flight providing assistance to the two Hornets damaged in a midair collision. Since whoever was behind this didn't expect Rattler to be on that flight, maybe that didn't factor into anything. Then there were the letters. Whoever was trying to help him or give him information seemed to think that maybe the email didn't get through so they resorted to writing letters. Clearly that was more difficult, but the question remained as to whether the person sending the email and letters was trying to help Rattler, or was actually part of the plot against him.

None of it added up, and Rattler kept coming back to the look on the skipper's face when he'd left his room. His comment came out as a joke, but the look in that man's eyes was sinister. Then Rattler saw him leaving with two men at the hotel just before Rattler's room was ransacked and Cheri assaulted. This was getting serious; Rattler needed answers quickly. Ever since he'd been young, Rattler never really worried about himself or about getting hurt, but when other people he cared about were threatened, that was a different matter.

Rattler needed to find out a few things before going any further. First off, where was Skipper during their port call in Dubai? Second, who set up the station for the Hawkeye the night Rattler and his crew were missile targets? He tried to think about the makeup of the three flight crews; he was the only common denominator. Sickboy and Clipper had been his copilots, and Shotgun had been in the back for the SAM incident.

Didn't Clipper say something about Shotgun and Skipper having an argument after the hydraulic issue? Rattler wondered.

Rattler thought about the people he could trust right now. He knew he could trust Clipper since they had been together forever, and there was no way he'd be dumb enough to sabotage things and then put himself in the aircraft when something bad happened. He might be able to trust Shotgun too since he seemed like a nice guy and he'd been put to the test during the SAM incident. Rattler finished getting ready. He knew he had to sit down with Clipper ASAP and figure this all out. Who was on whose side? How should they move forward? One thing was for sure: if Skipper was purposely trying to sabotage aircraft, Rattler would not rest until he was brought to justice.

He took one more look around the room, making a mental picture of where everything was, and then took the beer bottle off the door handle. It was time to get Clipper and head to the squadron party. As he opened the door to the hallway, which accessed only the two penthouse suites, Rattler felt a little more secure about where they were staying. The only way up here was by special key card, and there was no reason to be here unless you were staying in one of the two suites. The hotel had also agreed to send roving patrols up to the top floor. Rattler looked up at the cameras mounted in every corner of the hallway and nodded to himself. This was definitely safer, but he couldn't let his guard down.

CHAPTER 30

Clipper answered the door, ready for the party; Cheri needed a few more minutes. Clipper's mood had changed. He was either all party or all business and was definitely in business mode now. He didn't take well to Cheri being assaulted, and the thought of his life being at risk because of someone else's unethical scheme really bothered him. Clipper was one of the bravest pilots Rattler knew. He hoped to go on to be a test pilot after his Hawkeye tour, but even now he took calculated risks.

"Dude, my mind has been racing," Clipper said. "And Cheri's pretty upset."

"Can I ask you something before she comes out here, man?" Rattler asked quietly.

"Of course," Clipper replied.

"Can we trust her?"

Clipper took a minute to process the question. After meeting Cheri in Dubai, the two had stayed in close touch. In Clipper's mind, there was no reason to distrust her, but the navy had taught him that there were bigger things at play in life: other countries would often use women to obtain secrets from servicemen. While Clipper pondered all of this, he could hear her getting ready in the bedroom. He wanted this to be the start of a great relationship, but he also knew there would be risks. Before he could answer Rattler, there was a knock on the door.

"So much for no one knowing where we are," Clipper said.

"Check it out," Rattler replied.

As Clipper cautiously approached the door, Cheri came out of the bedroom. Clipper gave her the signal to be quiet. She walked over to Rattler as Clipper looked through the peephole in the door. Satisfied, he stepped back and opened the door.

"Room service, sir," the man said.

"I didn't order room service," Clipper replied, eyeing the cart full of fresh fruit, cheese, and high-end bottles of rum and vodka along with a bottle of chilled champagne.

"This is on the house, sir. I was told to bring this to you by the manager to help make up for the earlier misunderstanding," the man said.

Clipper looked at Rattler and shrugged as the man placed the cart in the room and promptly left. Clipper shut and locked the door behind him, then the three of them stood there in silence. Was this just a nice gesture from the hotel management, or was there more to it? Being paranoid wasn't going to help them, but with everything that had happened, suspicion was ever-present.

"So, are you two going to fill me in?" Cheri asked as she broke the silence in the room. "You know, Sandy is going to be here tomorrow, and she isn't going to be comfortable with all of this."

His mind crowded with other thoughts, Rattler had almost forgotten about Sandy and their plans to be together. He certainly didn't want to put her in harm's way and would have to be honest with her. Rattler nodded at Clipper who then went on to explain everything to Cheri. He went as far back as the hydraulic problem Rattler had dealt with in the aircraft. As he told the story, Cheri's expression went from shocked, to terrified, to determined. Once the initial shock had worn off, she wanted to help figure out what was going on. She didn't know the members of the squadron like Rattler and Clipper did, but an outside perspective can help bring clarity.

"What did you do to your skipper that caused him to hate you so much?" Cheri asked Rattler.

"He didn't do anything," Clipper intervened. "Rattler does things by the book and is one hell of a pilot."

"Then he clearly sees you as a threat to whatever he is trying to accomplish," Cheri replied. "At first, he was hoping to scare you into line, but now that he sees you actually standing in the way of his agenda, he is out to get you, and anyone near you."

"I'm so sorry about what happened to you in the hotel room," Rattler said.

"It's OK," Cheri replied. "I grew up in the back country of Australia, and I can take care of myself. I think I was upset because I wasn't expecting it and I let my guard down. Now that I know the backstory, I'm ready to help. And being aware, I can keep my eyes open. Remember, people often talk too much to pretty flight attendants," she said with a wink.

"OK, so what's our next move?" Clipper asked.

"You two have a squadron party to go to," Cheri said. "How about you go by yourselves, and I'll follow later. I can snoop around a little bit and listen to what people are saying. Maybe I can find some clues as to who else—if anyone—is behind this. Meanwhile, you two can act like everything is normal. Try to find Shotgun and see if he has any idea as to what's going on. Be careful, though, because if anyone else is involved and you tip them off, it could get really bad for us."

Both Rattler and Clipper nodded in agreement. It was tricky trying to figure out who they could trust, and who they couldn't.

"Cheri, I have to ask you something…" Rattler said. "Please don't take this personally, but can we trust you?"

"Yes, you can," Cheri said with a slight chuckle. "Because if I wanted you dead, you'd be dead already. Look, I like both of you, and I know how Sandy feels about you, Rattler. While this isn't the ideal way to start any relationship, this is what we have to deal with, so let's figure it out. We all want to be able to enjoy some time together before you both have to leave."

CHAPTER 31

Rattler and Clipper made their way down the elevator and through the hotel concourse to the banquet room next to the hotel bar. The squadron had rented the room to throw a party for the air wing. By the time they arrived, the party was in full swing. Rattler tried to take inventory of who was there, and more importantly, who wasn't. He saw Spike and Repeat at the bar, as well as most of the other members of the Wallbangers. Shotgun was talking to a waitress and looking pretty happy about it, but Rattler noticed that their skipper didn't seem to be there.

Months at sea without a proper port call can have a negative effect on an air wing. Since their last port call in Dubai, the air wing had been flying a lot and the operational tempo kept very high. Prior to that port call, the stresses had been the same. There is a direct correlation between operational tempo and how risky flying around the ship can be. Flying a lot can help minimize the risk in terms of added experience, but only to a point. CAG knew they were approaching that point of diminishing returns; his pilots were on edge, and they needed some time off.

"We stick together," Clipper said.

"Got it," Rattler replied. "Act normally, but always have an eye out for each other. Don't leave alone."

"Want a drink?" Clipper asked.

"Sounds good," Rattler replied as Clipper went to the bar, scanning the room along the way as if on a mission. Once again, Rattler reflected on Clipper's career. Clipper was an interesting individual who was not being used to his fullest potential by the navy. He could fly fighters with the best of them, but there hadn't been any fighter positions open when he'd finished flight school, so, like Rattler, he'd come to the Hawkeye community. Clipper's goals didn't stop at being a test pilot; ultimately, he wanted to be an astronaut. Rattler had no doubt in his mind that Clipper could achieve all that, and more. His only fault, if he had one, was that when he wasn't challenged, he became lazy. But all that had changed with the recent events, and as Rattler watched him at the bar, he knew that Clipper was laser focused.

"Having fun?" Shotgun asked, startling Rattler.

"Yes, sir," Rattler replied. "How have you been?"

"Knock off that 'sir' shit, man," Shotgun joked. "I'm happy to be off the ship like the rest of you. I bet you needed a break: you've been through a lot lately. How are you holding up?"

"Taking it one day at a time," Rattler replied. "I mean, things seem crazy, but I guess this is just deployment, right?"

"Three drinks!" Clipper said as he returned. "Shotgun, brother, I saw you over here so I got you this. How have you been doing with all this crazy shit?"

"Thanks, man, I appreciate that," Shotgun replied. "I'm OK, but being in charge of the maintenance department when you don't have a lot of support can be difficult."

"I bet, man," Clipper replied. "Crazy shit we have all been through… I feel like we're all on edge, but I honestly think it's like someone is working against us."

The three men looked at each other, trying to read each other. Rattler and Clipper trusted one another, but while they liked Shotgun, they didn't know how much he knew, or if he was involved. If he was involved, they would have to be careful until they figured out which side he was on. Rattler remembered that Shotgun was in the back of the Hawkeye during the missile attack, so it was unlikely that he was on the side of the bad guys. After another few moments of attempted mind reading, the silence was broken.

"We need to talk," Shotgun said. "But not here."

"OK let's go," Rattler agreed. "Where do you want to go?"

"To my room," Shotgun replied.

The three squadron mates left the banquet room without anyone noticing and made their way quietly to the elevator and up to Shotgun's room. He was a higher-ranking officer; instead of sharing accommodation, he'd requested a small room to himself. The three men entered the room, and Rattler and Clipper sat down.

"Listen, I am really risking it by telling you this, so I need to know that you will keep what I am about to tell you between us totally confidential," Shotgun began.

Rattler and Clipper nodded their agreement.

"OK, so I guess I have to go back to the beginning here. You know the skipper and I have a long history: he was my instructor at the RAG and brought me to this squadron once he knew he was going to take over. While I would not consider us friends, he always confided in me and seemed to be grooming me for eventual command of a Hawkeye squadron.

"Everything seemed to be going fine on this deployment until about two months ago. Skipper became more and more upset by CAG's infrequent use of the Hawkeye during combat operations. We told him that this deployment wasn't geared for the Hawkeye's expertise, but he wouldn't listen. He began talking irrationally about how it would take a plane getting shot down before the navy would put more money into the Hawkeye community. I mostly chalked his comments up to being on deployment and away from home. He has a family, and I'm sure that he misses them, but his ramblings couldn't be explained by that. I was busy sending him reports of the problems we were having with the planes, but instead of fixing these issues, he let maintenance items go unattended, almost like he wanted them to get worse."

"Hey, is that why I heard you say that skipper knew about the hydraulic problems with the Hawkeye that Rattler had to emergency land?" Clipper asked.

"Yes," Shotgun sighed. "That was the start of it. I was telling Skipper that we had a problem there, but he ignored it. I should have done more about that, but I was also hoping that port call in Dubai would help reset and recharge everyone's batteries. Maybe a fresh start was all we needed, but it just got worse. Normally, when we pull into port, the skipper and XO take the department heads out for dinner, but we didn't do anything. In fact, no one saw Skipper the whole port call.

"As you know, after we were all recalled to the ship, we went flying pretty quickly. The funny thing about it is that I expected the skipper to welcome that mission—it's what he'd been waiting for: an opportunity for the E2 to really shine, and honestly, solidify Skipper's reputation for a long time. It would make his career and get him his star, if he succeeded. That's why I thought it was weird that he immediately told me I was going to be the mission commander. He said he couldn't think of a better person for the job. Prior to that, he had stopped talking to me and kept to himself; I was surprised by that change in him."

"Did you decide where to station us that night?" Rattler asked.

"No," Shotgun replied after thinking about it. "Before I walked down to the mission-planning room, the skipper was adamant about where the Hawkeye would fly its station profile. I thought that was odd, but when I asked about the position, the skipper told me to follow his orders."

"Show him the letters," Clipper said to Rattler.

"What letters?" Shotgun replied.

Chapter 32

After Rattler showed Shotgun the letters he'd received and told him about the mysterious email, Shotgun looked shocked. He sat on his bed for a while trying to piece it all together. He had known the skipper for years and couldn't believe that he would be involved in such sabotage, but the signs were pointing that way. Shotgun knew that they had less than a week to figure it out because once they were back on the ship, the skipper was in charge and could easily put everyone at risk.

The three decided to go back down to the party to see if the skipper had shown up. As they rejoined the party, it was obvious that the wheels had completely come off. Most everyone in the air wing was there, including CAG and DCAG, and the crowd was having a blast, making it easy to split up, blend in, and look for clues. Clipper went to hang with the newer pilots in the squadron, taking on his usual, fatherly role. Shotgun found the other department heads and pretended to be interested in discussions around next promotions. He'd always found it funny that they acted like best friends when most were trying to get ahead in order to make the next career milestone. Rattler kept it simple and went to the bar. He wanted to find a relatively quiet vantage point where he could keep an eye on the comings and goings.

Sitting at the bar, Rattler knew he had to act soon. He had few resources in Australia, but he would have to make do. But before he made any big moves, he needed to know which side everyone was on. One blunder, or accusation involving the wrong person, and his career would be over. If Skipper had ignored the maintenance reports and put his crew at risk, then Rattler had him in his sights, career be damned.

Rattler thought back to the night he'd flown the Hawkeye with the flight control problems. Not only had someone likely sabotaged the system, but they also had to set it up so that the plane would fly correctly at the beginning of the flight. If a critical failure had occurred on the catapult shot, there wasn't a pilot in the navy who could have recovered; the plane and crew would be a total loss.

Rattler thought back to what he knew about the skipper's career. He'd attended Naval Academy and completed a successful junior officer tour, which got him an instructor job at the Fleet Replenishment Squadron. He then went on to a training officer tour, followed by his department head tour. As Rattler thought more about the skipper's history, chills went down his spine. He'd said that he was the maintenance officer during his department head tour: that experience alone would give the skipper intimate knowledge of aircraft systems, and possibly, the ability to bring about a critical system failure at just the right time.

The most significant question on Rattler's mind was whether or not the skipper intended for them to crash that night. The loss of an E-2C Hawkeye would be a major blow to the squadron, and the whole Hawkeye community. Each squadron only had four aircraft and with the amount each was worth, they were considered national assets. A Hawkeye crash for whatever reason would get a lot of attention from very high places. It would likely make the skipper look bad, unless he could cover up the maintenance problems and point to a bigger design flaw, or lack of funding and updates.

Skipper would always say that the aircrew is just a small part of the bigger picture and that we were all expendable. *Would he really kill five of his crew to prove his point?* Rattler ordered another drink and scanned the room again. Clipper was making his rounds, and Shotgun looked uncomfortable—which made sense since his mind was racing with newfound knowledge. Maybe it had been a mistake to tell Shotgun, but they needed more information. For the time being, they had to trust him and hope that he would help get to the bottom of this mystery. His drink refreshed, Rattler went back to trying to connect the dots.

For a moment, he allowed that the skipper had wanted the Hawkeye to crash. If so, Rattler had thrown a wrench into his plan by nursing that plane back aboard the ship, forcing the skipper to up his game. During the Dubai port call, unknown events changed the skipper for the worse. No one saw him during the port call, and then everyone was brought back to the ship on emergency recall. It seemed like a pretty big deal to recall all members of the ship and get underway so unexpectedly, and Rattler couldn't remember that ever happening to anyone else.

Before he knew it, he and Clipper had been tasked with a mission that CAG had directed him to fly. *Was CAG involved?* Rattler thought about that for a moment and had a hard time believing that CAG would be implicated. From the moment they'd met, CAG had seemed like the most patriotic person, one who would do anything for his country. Rattler truly believed that CAG's decision to put him on that mission was backed by honest motivations.; however, the fact remained that Shotgun was put in as mission commander, and Skipper had been adamant about where the Hawkeye was stationed. Given the radar range and communication limits of the aircraft, Rattler had found it odd to be so close to the action, but he had listened to what Shotgun told him. There was no doubt that Skipper had wanted them to fly in that particular area.

As Rattler was going over all this in his head, he scanned the hotel entrance and saw Cheri emerge from a door near the front desk. She was dressed to play the part, looking every bit like a model and sure to gain the attention of most men around. Rattler's mind drifted to both Cheri and Sandy—they represented another anomaly of the Dubai port call. Clipper said he'd met them at a bar and Rattler had no reason to disbelieve him; Clipper was good at talking to any woman anywhere. Cheri and Sandy seemed honest and were likely just looking to have fun, but he had a nagging fear that there was more to their chance acquaintance than what met the eye. Cheri saw Rattler at the bar and smiled and winked at him, but she made her way over to Clipper who was recounting a flying story to a group of new pilots. Cheri threw her arms around him and really hammed it up in order to make Clipper seem more impressive.

"Hey, sailor, I heard you're looking for a roommate." Rattler spun around on his barstool and there was Sandy. She was wearing her flight attendant's uniform and leaning on her rolling suitcase. Rattler was immediately shocked, and it showed. She wasn't due in town until late the following night. Rattler had already resigned himself to spending the night alone in his huge penthouse suite, most likely getting little sleep.

"You're here?" Rattler mumbled. "I thought you weren't getting back until tomorrow!"

"Well, it's not every day that a sexy, US Navy pilot pulls into port to visit, right? So maybe I said that I wasn't feeling good so that I could get off my trip and come here quicker. I went to the front desk to try to get to your room, but they said you aren't staying at the hotel. I was feeling completely dejected until I saw Cheri in the lobby. She pulled me into an office and told me that something's up, but that she wanted me to hear it from you. She told me you were at the bar, so I figured I would come find you. Are you not staying here?"

"It's a long story. I do have a very nice room, but it's not here. It's complicated," Rattler said.

"Is it another woman?" Sandy asked. "I can handle that, but you need to let me know."

"Heck, no!" Rattler replied. "That's the farthest thing from it, actually. As far as other women go, I am officially single now."

"That's great news," Sandy said, leaning in to kiss Rattler. "Why don't you show me this 'very nice' room, and then you can fill me in on whatever's going on. I've had a long day and need a bath. Does your room have a bathtub?"

"Yes, it does." Rattler smiled as he stood up, taking Sandy's suitcase in one hand and her hand in the other. Rattler caught Clipper's attention on the way out. Friends as close as Rattler and Clipper had the ability to communicate without words, and Rattler knew Clipper and Cheri would be safe as they kept working the party room.

Sandy was exhausted and opted to have a nap right away; Rattler sat in the chair next to the bed as Sandy slept. Afterward, they ordered some food and champagne and then went into the giant hot tub overlooking the city. Feeling that he could trust her, Rattler explained everything to Sandy as she listened intently. She offered no immediate insight and said that she wanted to sleep on it. Tomorrow morning, they would sit down over breakfast and come up with a plan. She made it clear that she was there for him in any way he needed, which made Rattler feel better. It had been ages since he'd had a caring woman in his life.

"Hey, come to bed and warm me up," Sandy said as she rolled over. "I didn't bring anything to sleep in and it's cold in here. A little body heat would help." Giggling, she pulled the sheets back. Rattler was no fool. He immediately put aside everything that was on his mind and crawled into bed. With a beer bottle on the door handle, he felt they were relatively safe, and for the first time in a long time, he relaxed.

CHAPTER 33

Rattler's eyes opened to the light shining through a gap in the curtains. He'd slept well and almost forgot where he was. He looked around the giant room, spotting Sandy's suitcase in the corner and hearing the shower running. He immediately felt better that she was there. He also hoped that this wasn't just a fling because he really liked Sandy. Obviously, she was beautiful, but it was more than that: she was everything Jennifer wasn't—confident, professional, and fun. She was proving to be a great listener and friend as well. Rattler could never have imagined himself in this situation, but here he was in a massive hotel suite in Australia with a beautiful woman, trying to keep everyone he was close to safe and figure out what was going on aboard the USS *Nimitz*.

He stood up to stretch and glanced at the door. The beer bottle was still sitting on the door handle. It was a dumb trick, but it made him feel more secure. He walked over to the main window, pulling back the curtain to reveal the morning sun and the vast city lying beneath him. He decided that Sandy came from an interesting place. Maybe it was the combination of city and country life so closely knit together, but it made for some great people who were hardworking, proud, and progressive all at once. As he was gazing out the window, he heard the shower water turn off. He made his way into the bathroom, still a little unsure of himself despite how close they had become in a short time. He peeked in to see Sandy drying off as she faced away from him. Her body was amazing. At his core, he was still very much a guy and a navy pilot, and the sight of a beautiful, naked woman made his heart race.

"Hey there, stud. I thought you were going to sleep all morning," Sandy said. She turned around and wrapped the towel around her body.

"You know spoiling a girl like this is not a good thing… I might just get used to it. Did you sleep well?"

"Yes, I did, and you deserve to be spoiled," Rattler said with a smile.

"Good," Sandy replied. "I know you've been through a ton of stuff lately, and being on the ship as a single person cannot be easy. After Dubai, all I wanted to do was spend more time with you. I have to admit that you are in my thoughts way more than I expected you to be. Maybe I shouldn't tell you that, but I had to get it off my chest so you know where I stand."

"I couldn't have said it better myself," Rattler whispered as he went over and hugged and kissed her. "Why don't you finish getting ready and order some breakfast. I'll shower and then we can sit down and you can tell me your thoughts on my current situation."

"Sounds great, but don't spend too much time in the shower or I'll be coming in there to get you," she teased.

Rattler jumped into the shower and even tried to make it quick, but in contrast to the no frills lifestyle aboard ship, a big, hot hotel shower always felt good. It was like he was trying to wash the ship life off. After he finished, he dried off and was throwing on some clothes when there was a knock on the door.

He emerged from the bathroom to see Sandy opening the door to the room service attendant who wheeled in a cart of food. Sandy was wearing a robe and had her hair wrapped up in a towel. She still looked amazing, but the room service attendant didn't seem to notice. She gave him a tip and he was gone. Rattler looked to the door handle and then at Sandy.

"I saw the same movie," Sandy said, holding the beer bottle. "I appreciate you trying to protect me, but remember, I'm a grown woman who has been all around the world. I can take care of myself… but thank you. Now, let's eat!"

They set up the food near the window to be able to enjoy the view. Both were very hungry and hardly spoke during the meal, but once they were finished, Sandy finally opened up about Rattler's situation.

"So, this is what I think," she said. "First, I want to thank you for trusting me. Most guys, especially the ones around here, would just freak out, close up, and not talk, especially since this—are we calling this a relationship?—is so new, and all."

"I think we can call it that," Rattler smiled.

"Well, it feels good to be around someone who genuinely cares about what I think," she continued. "From what you're telling me, I think your skipper is ultimately involved in this. Sounds like he's been in the navy too long and hasn't gotten enough recognition, so now he's purposely trying to make things hard on the squadron so that he can come in, fix everything, and look like a hero. While this may have started innocently enough, it's out of hand now, and he's in over his head—that's what scares me the most. Between the letters you got on the ship and what happened to Cheri in the hotel room, there's no telling how far the skipper will go."

"I agree," Rattler said as he got up to check his phone. "This deployment is almost over, and I'm wondering if he feels like this is his last chance to set himself up. He'll be turning over command shortly after we get home and will likely move to a desk job."

"Are you OK with Clipper and Cheri coming over?" Rattler asked, looking at his phone.

"Sure. Just give me ten minutes," Sandy replied. "I like Clipper, but he doesn't need to see me like this."

Chapter 34

After coming up with a plan, Rattler, Sandy, Clipper, and Cheri made their way to the hotel housing the rest of the squadron. Rattler and Sandy would try to trace the skipper's movements. Clipper and Cheri would split up, with Clipper looking for more information from Shotgun, and Cheri trying to find out who the two men were that Rattler had seen with the skipper. All four would keep their eyes open for the skipper because he'd been conspicuously absent from the squadron party.

The hotel lobby was pretty quiet—typical for this time of day given that an entire air wing was staying here and had been partying nonstop; hangovers were just starting to kick in. Rattler and Sandy sat down at the hotel restaurant to get a cup of coffee, and Rattler watched as pilots from the air wing came in from standing watch on the ship. As Rattler sipped his coffee, he was extra glad to be free from duty and was happy to be spending time with Sandy. There was something about her blonde hair and her confidence that made her very appealing to Rattler. She had traveled around the world, but for some reason, she seemed very content to be sitting here, sipping coffee and just enjoying time with him. Rattler wasn't used to such simple pleasures.

"Hey guys," Spike said, walking up. "How are you doing this morning?"

"Great!" Sandy replied. "How about you?"

"I'm pretty good. Got some good video chat in with the wife and kids, which helps me recharge my batteries. I need to run back to the ship and was going to meet Shotgun here this morning and ride back with him, but I haven't seen him yet," Spike explained.

Both Sandy and Rattler looked at each other, and the hair on the back of Rattler's neck stood up.

"When was the last time you saw him?" Rattler asked.

"Last night," Spike replied. "Didn't you hear? He and Skipper got into a huge argument in the lobby late last night. Most of the party was over, but I came back down to grab a quick snack before bed so I saw them. They were in the corner of the lobby, and whatever Skipper told Shotgun, he didn't like it. Honestly, man…I thought they were going to get into a fist fight."

"OK, well, we aren't doing anything, so we'll look for him," Rattler said. "Why don't you head to the ship and I'll text you when we find him?"

"OK, sounds good, brother," Spike replied. "Sandy, treat this guy good; he's saved my life more times than I can count."

"Will do." Sandy winked in return.

As Spike walked away, Rattler texted Clipper, telling him to meet them in the lobby. Clipper replied saying that it would take a few minutes to get back, but that he was on his way. Sandy texted Cheri who only replied that she was on to something and would touch base later. Both Rattler and Sandy were worried about Shotgun. If what Spike had seen lined up with what Rattler thought was going on, there was a good chance that Shotgun was in danger; Rattler only hoped it wasn't too late.

Clipper arrived and Rattler filled him in. They needed to find Shotgun immediately and warn him, but no one knew what room he was in. Clipper had an idea. Rattler and Sandy watched as Clipper approached the front desk, purposely avoiding the guy and heading straight to the slightly overweight female working at the opposite end of the desk. She looked shy and not very confident, but within seconds, she was smiling as Clipper struck up a conversation with her. Rattler could almost see her blush from across the room. Minutes later, Clipper was walking back to the table with a room key in hand and a smile on his face.

"Do I even want to ask?" Rattler asked.

"Do you need to, bro?" Clipper replied.

"No, you're right," Rattler said. "Sandy, why don't you stay down here while we check out Shotgun's room?"

"And miss all the excitement?" Sandy replied. "No way. Look, I'm in this with you two. I know I don't fly airplanes, and I also know how cocky pilots can be, but this is my home. If things are getting bad, you're going to need me close by to help out. I know people here and can help you. Plus, do you really want to leave a good-looking girl like me alone in the lobby with all these pilots walking around?"

"She's got a point," Clipper smiled.

"OK, let's go see if he's in his room," Rattler replied.

As they made their way up to Shotgun's room, Rattler had a bad feeling. If Skipper was really coming loose mentally and not thinking straight, there was no telling what he could do—not that he was a particularly big or physically fit man, but he did appear to be completely obsessed with his career. If his plan was to make a final stand, or do something to ensure that his name went down in history, Rattler feared it would not be in a positive way.

When they got to the room, Sandy agreed to wait out in the hallway. Rattler knocked on the door and waited, hoping that Shotgun would answer, but there was no response, so Clipper used the key to open the door.

At first glance, there were no signs of anything abnormal. Shotgun's uniform was hanging up in the closet, and his bag was on the floor. The door to the bathroom was slightly ajar and the light was on. Rattler called out to Shotgun before slowly opening the door. It became clear that Shotgun was never going to answer. He was lying in the bathtub, fully clothed, with three bullet holes in his chest and one in his head, his eyes gazing endlessly at the ceiling. Clipper came in behind Rattler and stopped in his tracks.

"Shit!" Clipper said.

"I'm sorry, sir," Rattler whispered. "I should have been able to stop this."

"This isn't your fault, man. We need to find the skipper. I think all of this points to him."

"I agree. So how do we handle this?" Rattler asked.

"Look, man, I'm all for walking away, but the girl at the desk knows I asked for a key to this room. She knows we're up here, and I'm guessing there are security cameras too. This isn't the time to try to cover this up. We need to report it and find Skipper," Clipper replied.

As Clipper and Rattler walked out of the room to find Sandy and tell her what had happened, the elevator doors opened and Skipper was there. He looked briefly at the three of them and then before Rattler could say a word, he immediately closed the elevator doors.

"Stay with Clipper!" Rattler told Sandy as he sped off for the stairs.

CHAPTER 35

His heart racing, Rattler ran down the ten flights of stairs down to the lobby. It was all coming together now: not only was the skipper involved, but he was directly linked to Shotgun's death, and most likely, to all the other worrisome events too. Shotgun had a wife and kids; there was no way Rattler was going to let Skipper get away. When he got to the lobby level, Rattler saw Skipper running out the front door of the hotel. He resumed the chase, nearly knocking over an elderly couple as he turned left to follow the skipper down the street. There was no doubt now that the skipper was trying to evade Rattler.

Dodging the crowds on the sidewalk, Rattler was gaining on Skipper, but he didn't know how long he could keep it up. The skipper made a hard left turn down another street, and Rattler felt a surge of energy. This man had tried to kill him and his friends and had something to do with Shotgun's death. Rattler owed it to all of them to catch him. To his dismay, he saw Skipper jump into a familiar-looking black SUV, and before he could reach it, it sped away.

Rattler stopped to catch his breath. Obviously, the skipper had been heading to Shotgun's room and didn't expect to see Clipper and Rattler there. Whatever his plan, it had clearly changed now, and Rattler, Clipper, and Sandy were no longer safe. Walking back to the hotel, Rattler reflected on the close calls he'd managed to survive in recent weeks. He could feel his blood pressure rising as he realized that the man tasked with leading him safely into combat had actually been trying to kill him.

Rattler neared the hotel, and he could see multiple police cars out front, as well as an ambulance. The lobby was no longer quiet but had become a sea of people and nervous energy. He walked through the crowd and Rattler saw Clipper and Sandy talking to a police officer. Clipper saw him first and hurried over to close the distance.

"Dude, play along," Clipper said.

"Huh?" Rattler replied.

"Hello, sir. Is your name Jack Owen?" the police officer asked.

"Yes, sir," Rattler replied.

"We're going to have to take you down to the station for questioning," the officer stated.

"OK. Can I just go up to my room and get a change of clothes?" Rattler asked.

"No. I don't think you understand, sir. I am taking you to the station in connection with the death of LCDR Mike Anderson." The officer pulled out handcuffs.

Rattler's first instinct was to panic, but he looked over at Clipper, who nodded that it was OK. Aircrew filled the lobby in time to see Rattler being handcuffed and escorted to a police car. Clipper and Sandy followed. Once outside, the two of them made their way to another police vehicle.

"Thanks, bro. We will see you at the station," Sandy said to the officer as he carefully guided Rattler into the back of his car.

"No problem, kiddo. Just be careful," he replied.

Rattler's head swam with thoughts once again. *What the hell is going on?* He felt like he could barely keep up. Not long ago, he'd found his squadron mate dead, seemingly execution style, and then he'd frantically given chase to the skipper whose menacing involvement was deepening by the hour. Now he was in the back of a police car, trying to figure out the connection between Sandy and this officer. *Why did they make such a show out of arresting me in the lobby?* Clipper and Sandy knew he'd nothing to do with Shotgun's death. He wanted to believe this was all a show, but he was anxious nonetheless.

Instead of asking the officer what was going on, Rattler decided to fight the urge and remain quiet. He hoped that Clipper was on his side, but wasn't even sure of that anymore; he just wanted to protect himself. As he sat in the back of the police car, still sweating through his clothes, it was clear to him that the skipper wasn't the only one involved. Rattler also needed to figure out who had sent him the various warnings.

The police car raced along, and Rattler hoped that Clipper and Sandy were also headed to the police station so that they could get to the bottom of this together. He lay back and closed his eyes, dreaming of flying and out of the clouds. He longed to be in the sky, where he felt in control; he missed those days already.

Chapter 36

Sitting next to the workbench in a mechanic shop in New Jersey, a young Jack Owen watched quietly as his father looked over the 1979 Pontiac Firebird. Like a surgeon looking over a patient, he checked every possibility. Jack had a great deal of respect for his father. He may not have been like other fathers, but he taught Jack a good many things, whether he realized it or not.

It was summertime and the temperature inside the shop was stifling. His dad worked in blue pants and a short-sleeved, button-down mechanic shirt that had his name and the name of the shop embroidered over the chest. Jack watched his dad's every move and tried to mimic them. His father was a kind man; Jack knew that kindness was one of the reasons that his mother loved him so much. Jack looked over his shoulder to see his mother on the phone at the front desk of the shop, writing something into the calendar. It was long past closing time, but they were both still working long hours to make ends meet.

Jack's father was explaining what he was looking at on the car and how he thought he'd figured out the problem, but Jack heard none of it. Earlier that year, the family had visited Long Island to see an airshow featuring the US Navy Blue Angels flight demonstration team. Ever since that day, Jack couldn't forget the sight of those speedy blue jets flying inches apart. Genetic makeup and natural ability had led Jack to think of a career in professional football, but there was something in those jets—something intoxicating that grabbed a hold of him and wouldn't let go.

Jack didn't know the first thing about the navy, or flying for that matter, and had no idea who to ask for guidance. While his father and uncle had both been in the air force, they were mechanics and didn't have any pilot friends. As a young boy sitting in New Jersey, dreaming of a future of high G-forces and traveling on aircraft carriers to the far reaches of the world's oceans, Jack felt that there was little to no chance of his dreams coming true.

"Dad, can I ask you a question?" Jack finally said.

"Sure," his dad replied, looking up from the engine bay. He stopped working on the car.

"Do you remember those blue, navy jets we saw in Long Island?" Jack asked.

"The Blue Angels? Yes, I remember," his dad replied.

"Is there any chance… I mean, do you think I could ever do that?" Jack quietly asked, his eyes trained on the floor.

"Listen, son." His dad put down the tools and came to stand beside him. "There isn't a thing on this planet that you can't achieve if you put your mind to it. This world has a way of trying to keep people down. It reminds you every day of the things you CAN'T do, but it is up to you to remember what you *can* do. This world can be brutal, and it will chew you up if you let it. I know you get bored when your mother and I have to work, but we are chasing our dream too. If flying jets for the navy is what you want to do, then don't let anyone—and I mean anyone—tell you that you can't do it. Never take no for an answer when following your dreams."

Rattler was startled by voices outside the door as he sat in a room with a few chairs and a metal desk. No one had come to talk to him yet, and he was losing track of how long he'd been there. At least they'd taken the handcuffs off when he arrived and given him a cup of coffee. He tried to stay calm and focused; he'd had been through plenty in his life and getting worked up about it never helped. His father's advice still in his head, Rattler's head cleared and he began to feel like his old self again. Determined to get through this so that he could get home and have a beer with his dad, he looked up as there was a sharp knock on the door.

CHAPTER 37

The door opened and the same officer from the hotel entered along with another man wearing a black suit. From head to toe, he looked like someone out of a movie: clean-cut and professional, but a man with a purpose who didn't have time for bullshit. Clipper and Sandy followed behind. She smiled when she saw Rattler and he returned the smile. After them came CAG and XO Spool. They all sat down at the table with the two officers, plus CAG and XO opposite Rattler, and Clipper and Sandy next to him.

Tension hung in the air as once again, Rattler felt his career was done. He was in a foreign land, essentially in jail: this realization had shaken him, but the full gravity of the situation had yet to be understood. Rattler sat in his chair and remembered what his father had told him about looking confident. He was completely unnerved now but hoped that no one would notice.

"Jack, my name is Officer Jared Jones and this is Officer Travis Smith. I'm sure that you are a bit confused as to what is going on, and I have to admit we were too. Luckily for you, Sandy and I grew up on the same street and when she called me for help, I knew that my academy roommate, Travis, would be the best one to assist us," the officer said, motioning to the man in the black suit who nodded back. "The situation is very delicate, and I think it's best to explain to you that first and foremost, you are not being held under formal charges at this point. While things are changing very quickly, I think it's best if Captain Grogan explains what is going on."

With this, CAG stood up. He had Rattler's full attention, as always. It didn't matter whether he was in his flight suit or civilian clothes, flying or on the ground; the man known around the squadron as "Nails" commanded respect, and this time was no different.

"How are you doing, son?" CAG asked.

"As good as I can be I guess, sir." Rattler couldn't muster much confidence.

"Listen… As Officer Jones explained, the situation is very fluid, and I'm going to give you the no-shit brief right now and get you up to speed. We have no time to waste, and everyone in this room has been read into the situation. Frankly, son, if they aren't in this room right now, I wouldn't trust them." CAG paused.

"Yes, sir," Rattler replied as he looked at Sandy who gave him a wink.

"Your skipper is a traitor, a bad American, and frankly, a piece of shit," CAG began. "I know you two have not always gotten along, and I'm here to tell you that your instincts were correct. Since taking over command, he has constantly been in my office asking me for more funding for the Hawkeye. Now, son, I have no problem asking big navy for more money—God knows they have it—but the things that your skipper wanted that money for didn't add up. They seemed geared toward personal career enhancement as opposed to bringing the Hawkeye community into an advanced tactical state. This has been going on a long time, but every time we spoke, I told him that I needed to see proof that the money was needed. Eventually, he took means into his own hands."

CAG went on to talk about how the skipper sabotaged Rattler's plane on cruise months ago, which would have resulted in it crashing on the flight deck if Rattler hadn't handled the landing so well. He then spoke about the port call in Dubai and the emergency recall to the ship, which was the result of intelligence of a pending attack on US assets. Finally, he spoke about the SAM incident and how Skipper was linked to that. He'd given the terrorists the exact location of the Hawkeye that night in an attempt to get rid of Rattler and Shotgun, the two biggest barriers to his plan. The rest of the crew and the plane would have just been collateral damage.

As CAG spoke, Sandy got a firsthand account of everything that Rattler had been through since they'd met. She held his hand under the table and squeezed tighter and tighter. Rattler split his attention between CAG and looking at Sandy and Clipper sitting on either side. Sandy's eyes reflected love; she had a growing admiration for Rattler, a man who she was just getting to know. Clipper, on the other hand, had hate-filled eyes. He would go to the end of the world for his squadron mates; now that he was learning the extent of Skipper's efforts to kill him, all loyalty had been crushed. Clipper was now a man on a mission to take down this tyrant.

CAG then came to the latest news. "Shotgun is dead." CAG's words echoed in Rattlers' heart.

"Yes, sir." Rattler was still coming to grips with it. Shotgun had a family at home—a wife and kids who loved him. They were likely getting the news now, but would they ever really know the truth behind his death?

"That brings you up to speed on everything that has happened so far. Any questions?" CAG asked.

"No, sir," Rattler replied.

"Good. Now, let's get to your most important mission yet. I need you to go back to the ship and do your best to act like nothing is wrong. Intelligence tells me that the skipper has linked up with a terrorist organization called the Palestinian Islamic Jihad (PIJ) with the goal of selling Hawkeye-capability secrets in exchange for shooting one down. Your job is to assist the XO in getting two Hawkeyes airborne. The plan is to have you fly one with the skipper as the mission commander in the back. The other Hawkeye will be piloted by Clipper with a full crew. The key here is that for the short time between now and the mission, I need Clipper to continue acting out against the skipper without letting on that he knows anything."

"Done! Fuck that guy!" Clipper interrupted.

"Rattler, I need you to befriend the skipper," CAG continued.

"Excuse me, sir?" Rattler replied.

"This is the way I see it: Skipper views you as his greatest threat. I need you to befriend him so that he will fly with you. Get his sights set on Clipper instead, but don't let on that you really know anything. Once you are both airborne, we will actually target your Hawkeye instead of

Clipper's. Our hope here is that Skipper will be frightened into revealing his plan. We can get it all recorded, and then lock him up for a long time."

"Sir, not to be the skeptical one in the room, but I have two concerns. First getting the skipper to think I like him, and second, the fact that my Hawkeye will be targeted," Rattler said.

"Well, son, your XO will help you with the first part, and the second one shouldn't worry you. You're the only Hawkeye pilot who can say that he's defeated a SAM!" CAG joked. "But in all seriousness, we plan to have a SEAL Team intercept the members of the PIJ, neutralize the threat, and take over to make it look and sound like the skipper's plan is working. I will leave you with this, son. You took an oath to defend against all enemies, foreign and domestic. I know that on that day, you never thought this would be your mission, but make no mistake: this is the most important mission you've had up to this point. We're counting on you to bring the skipper down before he does more damage to national security and causes more loss of life."

CHAPTER 38

"The view is pretty amazing," Sandy said from the hot tub with the bubbles barely covering her body. "You should come join me."

Rattler smiled in return. "I'm sorry that I got you involved in this. Life seemed so simple before, but listening to CAG talk about all that has gone on during this deployment makes me realize how crazy it has gotten. I'm really sorry that you are now roped into this."

"Listen, you didn't rope me into anything. It's not your fault that I'm attracted to strong men who exude the cowboy spirit. Listening to your CAG speak about everything you've been through was amazing. And being with a pilot is interesting because we never really get to see you do your job. Sure, you talk about it and the stories are great, but we cannot live it firsthand. CAG seems like a man who has lived through a lot, and if you can impress him, that speaks volumes," Sandy assured him.

"Thanks," Rattler said.

"Here's the thing though: I may not understand everything about your job, but I do understand that CAG could have chosen other pilots for this mission, but he chose you. Now is not the time to second-guess yourself. You have gotten to this place because you act. You are a confident pilot who handles whatever is thrown at him. Your country, your squadron mates, and your friends need you now, so stand tall and be the man who CAG believes you are. You can worry about all the 'what-ifs' later when we're sitting on a beach someplace, having a drink," Sandy smiled.

Rattler smiled as he looked out at the skyline view from the hotel window. He knew in his heart that Sandy was right. Now was not the time to second-guess the future; he had no choice but to roll with it, fall back on his training, and believe that in the end, it would all work out. He also knew that he only had a couple more days in port with Sandy before the ship got back underway, and he wanted to make the most of it.

The upcoming mission was going to be dangerous, and that was if he even managed to live long enough to get to that point. The skipper and his PIJ allies had clearly shown that they would kill to protect their interests, and Rattler had to assume that he was still in their sights. Maybe the skipper was shaken a little now, or maybe he was a crazed maniac who wouldn't stop until he got what he wanted. Rattler decided it didn't matter; he was going to enjoy his time in port like it was his last because it might very well be.

He and Sandy were going to hit a couple of night clubs and bars that night and meet up with members of the air wing. His first job was to pretend that nothing was abnormal, which wasn't going to be easy, but it was part of the bigger mission. Life could be harder though. Sitting in a hot tub inside a massive penthouse suite with a beautiful, naked Australian flight attendant was pretty easy to take. If only they had put this in the Naval Aviation Recruiting pamphlet…there would never be a pilot shortage again.

"Thank you," Sandy said, breaking the silence.

"For what?" Rattler asked.

"I know that you've been through a lot, even before all this. Dealing with a divorce and losing trust in your ex could not have been easy. Being out here on deployment, away from home, and having to deal with that would be too much for many people to handle. Then, here I come in Dubai and you treat me with the greatest respect and honesty, which you could have easily not done. I wouldn't even have faulted you if you had lied to me about everything just to protect yourself, but you didn't. From our first rooftop meeting, you were honest—even when you probably thought it would kill all your chances with me. That takes a lot of integrity. That is a quality that I find very sexy in a man. You had every opportunity to hide the truth from me, but that thought never crossed your mind. I just want to make sure you know how much that means to me," Sandy explained.

"Well, it wasn't all that hard," Rattler joked as he began to take off his clothes before getting into the hot tub. "I mean, you're a very nice woman to be around."

The doorbell rang, stopping Rattler in his tracks. Just as things had been starting to feel normal, his heart was racing again. He motioned for Sandy to stay put as he made his way to the door. He looked through the peephole to see who it was and saw Clipper on the other side. He cracked the door open slightly.

"Dude, if we're going to fucking die, we're going out with a bang. Get ready to party tonight," Clipper said.

"I wouldn't want it any other way. Give me an hour to get ready?"

"You got it, bro, and I just wanted to say that if I had to go through this shit with anyone, I'm glad it's you," Clipper said.

"I'll take that as a compliment. We will get through this… Can you imagine the windfall we're going to make off the movie rights to this story?" Rattler joked.

"Yeah, that would be great—if it wasn't going to be classified at the highest level. Meet me downstairs in an hour and bring that smoke show gal of yours," Clipper replied. Rattler shut the door.

CHAPTER 39

"Sweepers, sweepers man your brooms..." echoed over the 1MC.

Rattler groaned as he rolled over in his small bed onboard the ship. He was still feeling the effects of what seemed to be days of partying, and his head was foggy to say the least. He'd definitely made the best of his time with Sandy but was paying for it now. Back onboard the ship, life would get back to normal for most, but his life would remain unsettled until the special mission was over.

He hauled himself out of bed and took inventory of the room; it looked like everyone else had already left for the day and he was alone. After a quick birdbath at the sink and a shave, he sat down at his desk. With his flight suit half on and tied around his waist, Rattler toyed with the paperwork in front of him. He picked up the top piece of paper and read through it one more time. As he read, his mind went back through the years of his life. At only twenty-eight, his life seemed long already. From growing up, to wanting to be a pilot, to meeting the person he thought was the love of his life, it all just seemed like a blur.

Ever since the day he'd decided to fly for the navy, the only path to follow was that of a fighter pilot: that was the absolute tip of the spear and the pinnacle of navy pilot aspirations. As he sat there at his desk, reading the words that could make that dream come true, Rattler was torn. Did he sign the paper, seal the envelope, and deliver it to CAG? Doing so would open him up to the chance of failing again. Perhaps he should throw it away and move on with his life. Maybe being a fighter pilot wasn't his destiny.

The navy had realized that they were short of junior officers in the strike fighter community, and in an effort to fix that, they were opening up one board to allow pilots from other communities to apply to transition to the F/A-18 Hornet or Super Hornet. While Rattler had known other pilots who made a transition in their career, it was extremely rare and usually the result of a certain aircraft community going away and the navy needing to send their pilots somewhere else. This was the first he had heard of it being voluntary, and when he'd been approached by CAG weeks ago, it seemed like a simple decision. CAG went over the process and the pros and cons but ended by saying that both he and the skipper would not only endorse, but personally recommend his package for transition. At the time, Rattler had felt honored that two seasoned fighter pilots felt strongly enough about his drive and ability to put their names on the line to back his dreams.

Of course, a lot had changed in the past few weeks, and Rattler's mind was just starting to slow down and focus on the mission ahead of him. Part flying, part deception, and part flushing out what could be called a domestic terrorist, Rattler was ready to step up and serve his country. He was ready to ensure that his skipper would never hurt anyone again, but he had honestly not thought about the Hornet transition, and now it was time to decide.

On the one hand, Rattler's newly single life would make it easy to undergo training and deployments around the world. CAG had been very specific when he spoke about the timeline for the transition. Rattler had been on a "sea" tour for almost three years, and in the normal progression of the navy, it was almost time for him to rotate to a land-based job to allow him to recharge his batteries. If he was accepted for the transition, that time would be cut short or not exist at all. He would go and learn how to fly the Hornet and then be assigned right away to a sea-deploying squadron. While it had been done before, CAG wanted to make sure Rattler understood the hardship he would endure from that.

While being single would make it easier, Rattler would have less time to spend with his mother and father, and much less time to relax. Additionally, the timing of a career navy officer was very specific; if Rattler signed that paper, he would be throwing a huge wrench in the system and taking a huge career risk. There would be a very good chance that he would not be promoted the same way that he would if he stayed in the Hawkeye community. On the other hand, he was being offered a rare opportunity that was difficult to pass up.

Rattler leaned back in his chair and closed his eyes, thoughts of his childhood racing through his mind. Words of encouragement from his father echoed in his head. The same drive and determination that had propelled him to this point began to build again. He did not shy away from challenge; his career up to this point had already been unorthodox, and he couldn't worry about what his squadron mates might think. At the end of the day, he had to look himself in the mirror and know that he'd done what was right for him. His mother would worry, but she was so very proud of everything he had accomplished so far; she was his biggest supporter, and he didn't want to let her down.

Rattler opened his eyes. A single piece of paper lay there with a pen. He had no idea what would happen with the upcoming mission, and whether or not he would even survive, but one thing was for sure, he wasn't going to live a life of regrets. He picked up the pen, signed his name, placed the paper in the yellow envelope containing all the rest of the required documents, and sealed it. He had no idea what the future held, but he had taken the first step down a new path.

Success or failure was out there, and he would deal with it as it came, but right now, he needed to focus on the mission. A newfound strength came with signing that paper. While the Hawkeye did not have conventional weapons, Rattler knew that if successful, his actions would ensure the safety of those around him. He would not let them down.

CHAPTER 40

The team of people Rattler could trust was very small. From the moment he dropped off his transition package at the mail room, he was focused and taking inventory of those around him. Those in the know included CAG, XO, and Clipper. As for the rest, he had to watch what he said and did. For the majority of the squadron, it had been a horrible port call where Shotgun had accidentally fallen in the shower and broken his neck. The squadron was in mourning, and a missing man flyover and ceremony were being planned. Rattler didn't know when the undercover flight mission would happen, but CAG and XO said to expect sooner rather than later. They needed to act quickly to ensure that no more secrets were leaked and no one else got hurt.

Rattler entered the ready room, taking in the scene. Sickboy was standing SDO while the TV played the annual army/navy football game. The skipper, a Naval Academy graduate, wouldn't miss the game and was the only one watching. Rattler felt a white-hot sense of rage as Skipper sat there, eating popcorn like a child. Days ago, this man's actions had resulted in someone close to Rattler being murdered. There were children and a grieving widow who would never see their father and husband again, and there he sat as if nothing had happened. For a moment, Rattler thought about walking up behind the skipper and choking the last breath out of him, but he restrained himself. He had a mission to complete with strict orders from his CAG and XO. He would execute those orders to the best of his ability; it was game time all right.

"Hey, sir, how are you?" Rattler said as he walked up.

"Great. Greatest football game of the year…can't believe more people aren't watching it," Skipper replied. He was wearing a Naval Academy shirt and eyed Rattler with skepticism.

"Yeah, sir—I think everyone is just recovering from the port call and trying to get back into the swing of things aboard the ship," Rattler replied.

"That's the problem with you junior officers: you only care about drinking and partying, not naval tradition or the bigger picture," Skipper said.

Rattler suppressed his desire to rip the man apart. "Well, sir, I can't speak for this tradition since the Naval Academy didn't accept my application, but I understand what you're saying." Rattler attempted to change the subject and probe just a little. "Tragic about Shotgun, huh?"

Skipper turned to face Rattler for the first time since he'd entered the room. Would he be able to befriend Skipper? He had no idea how much the skipper knew or had pieced together. Their game of cat and mouse at the hotel, the unpleasant past they shared…going forward, everything hinged on this moment. Rattler would soon know whether the skipper was exceedingly stupid, or just too confident in his plan.

"It really is, but it just goes to show you that life is short and we have limited time on this planet to make a difference and effect change. You have to take every opportunity to set up your legacy when you can; otherwise, it may be over before you know it and then, what have you contributed to this place?"

"I couldn't agree more, sir." Rattler was armed and ready to bring down this tyrant. "How is your work on the Hawkeye recording and data link system going?"

With that, the skipper lit up. Rattler had needed to show only the slightest interest in his pet project for the befriending process to begin. Skipper went on and on about the program and how he needed to show the navy that the Hawkeye was the forgotten community. In order to truly make naval aviation complete, the Hawkeye community had to be brought up to speed. He spoke about how the plane was originally designed to be a long-range radar platform to find Russian bombers, but that in modern times, the Hawkeye could do so much more. Skipper saw it as his job to make sure the navy knew its capabilities and what it lacked; otherwise, there was a chance that the community would eventually be phased out.

It was clear to Rattler that the skipper thought his legacy would be that of the man who gave longevity to the Hawkeye community; without his actions, the navy would move on. Rattler now understood that anyone who got in Skipper's way was expendable and that this delusional man would stop at nothing to ensure the future of the Hawkeye. Rattler had taken in all he could for now. If he didn't end this conversation quickly, he would snap.

"Hey, Rattler—Grins just called and he needs you in the CAG Paddles office," Sickboy said.

"OK," Rattler replied. "Sir, let's talk about this more later. I have to run. Go navy, beat army!" Rattler managed to say as he held back both his rage and the vomit forming in his throat. Skipper had bought it all—hook, line and sinker. Rattler walked away.

"What was that all about?" Sickboy asked as Rattler walked past.

"Long story, buddy. Long story…" Rattler replied.

CHAPTER 41

Rattler knocked on the door to the LSO office and it was immediately opened. Inside the small office, he found CAG, XO, and Clipper.

"The mission is a go," CAG said as Rattler closed the door.

Rattler sat down as CAG went over the basics. They would launch in thirty-six hours: two Hawkeyes, a division of Hornets, a Prowler, and two Super Hornets for tanking assets. The plan would be simple, and CAG was going to let the skipper be the overall mission commander in an effort to give him enough rope to hang himself. On the surface, the mission was a set up to catch Skipper in the act of espionage, but in all other respects, it was real. There would be a SEAL team to intercept the members of the PIJ; it appeared that the skipper was still giving them classified information.

The idea was that Skipper would likely tell the PIJ where the Hawkeyes would be stationed, and then have them attempt to shoot one down. In Skipper's eyes, when that plane was hit, it would be the evidence needed to go to the navy and get more funding for the Hawkeye. The other Hawkeye, with Skipper in the back, would be safely out of the way. He would run the whole mission, and ultimately the search and rescue, becoming the hero. The mission played on Skipper's ego and was simple enough that it should work. Rattler worried that the members of PIJ would not be intercepted in time. No one in the two Hawkeye aircraft would know if the Navy SEALs had actually gained control before launching. They could very well fly right into the lion's den.

"Here's where we flip it on your skipper," CAG continued. "The plane with the skipper in the back will be the one targeted. I think that when he faces his demise, Skipper will crack and confess."

"Yes, sir." All Rattler could do was have faith in the plan.

"So, let's talk about the crews: Skipper will be in your Hawkeye with Repeat and Spike in the back, Rattler. The second Hawkeye will be flown by Clipper with a full crew. Here is the thing, though… The only people who will truly know what's going on once airborne will be you and Clipper. I'm asking your crews to walk into danger no differently than any other mission, and while I have considered briefing everyone else involved, there is too much risk that the skipper will find out.

"XO, you will be in CATCC and monitor everything here. I need you to be the eyes and ears of the whole operation and be ready to flex at a moment's notice. Everyone's safety is my top concern, and I want all aircraft back on deck in one piece, but I also want Skipper locked up for life. Any questions?"

"Am I launching in the second Hawkeye as bait to be shot down?" Clipper asked.

"Yes. Is that a problem?" CAG asked.

"No, sir. I just wanted to know what I'm getting into. Let's bag this asshole," Clipper affirmed.

"Sir, who will be my copilot?" Rattler asked.

"Me," CAG replied. "I spent four hours talking to your skipper about the Hawkeye and how much I agree it needs funding. I told him I'd welcome the opportunity to fly in it and see it in action firsthand. Let me be clear: I'll be there to keep an eye on him and to help you as much as I can. If shit hits the fan, I am not trained on the Hawkeye, so if you would rather have a copilot who is fully mission qualified, I understand."

"No, sir—I'd be honored to fly with you," Rattler replied.

"OK, gentlemen. This has been briefed at the highest level, and there are many moving parts. Make no mistake: I have zero respect for your skipper, and it is my number one goal to see him hang. Rattler, hang back; everyone else is dismissed."

As Clipper and the XO got up to leave, both men seemed laser-focused on what they had to do. Rattler felt for the XO, trying to imagine what it would be like to take down one's boss. If successful, he would immediately become the skipper. Clipper walked out of the room like a man on cloud nine. He'd always wanted to be the tip of the spear, and like many Hawkeye pilots, he wanted to fly fighters. He knew this would be the closest he'd get for a while; nevertheless, it was his time to show what he was made of and he was excited for the challenge. After they'd left, CAG closed the door and sat down opposite Rattler.

"Son, I know this is a lot to deal with. You've already rewritten history, and make no mistake, when you get home from this deployment, things are going to be different. Now I'm asking you to do it again: to put yourself in harm's way and go out there with no defenses while a fellow officer tries to get you and your friends killed. I know this isn't something you thought about when you signed up for this job. We talk about defending our country against all enemies, foreign and domestic, but we never think the threat will come from our own squadron mates, let alone the man who is supposed to be your leader.

"You have handled yourself in a manner that, frankly, I don't think I would have had the maturity to do at your age, and I'm proud of you. That being said, if you don't want to do this, I understand; I will find another pilot to take your place. This is going to be a dangerous mission. If the Navy SEALs don't get there in time, it's possible that both Hawkeyes will be at the bottom of the ocean before this is over."

"Sir, may I speak freely?" Rattler asked.

"Of course," CAG replied.

"Sir, you have been a fighter pilot for twenty-seven years. You have a family at home and have been putting your ass on the line for almost three decades in the service of your country. Everything you need to know about the Hawkeye you can learn on the ground, or be briefed on by your intelligence folks; yet, you are putting your ass in the right seat of my plane.

"I've learned a lot in the past couple months about myself, my squadron, and what real leadership is. Frankly, you putting yourself out there on this mission shows me the type of leader I want to be. I know how to fly this plane to the edge of the envelope, and you couldn't get me out of that plane if you tried. Let's take this asshole down!" Rattler said.

CAG smiled and stood up. "You got it, son. Now remember who knows what about the mission and keep it quiet. Also, I hate to have to say this, but if you have anyone at home you want to say goodbye to, now is a good time to go write that letter."

CHAPTER 42

Rattler had been told about these letters before, and he hated the idea behind them. Thinking about your own death seemed to distract from the mission, and he'd never been in the position of needing to write one before, but things were different this time. CAG had been around a long time and likely had written a few such letters in his career. If he suggested writing it, then Rattler was going to do it. The question was, who would be the recipient?

Clearly, Jennifer didn't care about him anymore and writing to her would be a waste of paper. He'd become very close to Sandy over the last couple of months, but it seemed too early to write something like this to her. The only people who came to mind were Rattler's parents, mainly his mother. While both of his parents had always been there for him, his mother was his biggest fan. She wore a necklace each day with small navy wings on a pendant, and the gesture brought him closer to her. Rattler hated the thought of leaving her behind. He closed his eyes, focused his thoughts, and began to write.

Dear Mom and Dad,

If you are reading this, then the mission I am about to go on didn't go very well. I want to thank you both for giving me every opportunity in life to obtain my goals. I want to thank you for never giving up on me, regardless of what ideas I had or paths my life took me down. I know leaving home for college and being far away from you was not easy, but I thank you for allowing me to chase those dreams. I have made many mistakes along the way, but the guidance you raised me with always got me back on the right path. The mission I am going on is one that would make you both proud. It is dangerous but necessary, and I would not want anyone else to do it in my place. You taught me the difference between right and wrong and good and bad, and right now, as I sit here at my desk in my room aboard the ship, I am laser-focused on those things. While my life may have to be sacrificed to stop evil, know that in doing so, many lives have been saved. Please do not cry because I am gone. Hold your head up high knowing that I did what was right and hopefully made a difference. I will always look over you and can't wait to see you again. Love, Jack

Rattler picked up the letter, folded it, and placed it in an envelope in his desk. As he was closing his locker, the door opened. Clipper, Repeat, and Spike came in.

"Hey, guys, sit down," Rattler said.

"Everything OK?" Spike asked.

"Yes," Rattler replied.

"You sure you want to tell them?" Clipper asked.

"Very sure," Rattler replied. "Guys, what I am about to tell you is going against a direct order from CAG, but in my opinion, it's only fair that you know. We have been through a lot together, and I know I can trust you."

Rattler went on to lay out everything that had been going on behind the scenes, including the first SAM to hit a Hawkeye, the truth about what happened to Shotgun, the mysterious notes, the men in black suits, and everything that was planned for the upcoming mission. In Rattler's mind, Spike and Repeat were owed an explanation. They were going to be sitting on either side of a crazy tyrant who would stop at nothing, including sacrificing innocent lives, in order to ensure his legacy.

After Rattler had finished speaking, he paused and looked at both Spike and Repeat. He reiterated that everything he'd just explained was known only by himself, Clipper, CAG, and the XO, and that CAG and XO must never find out that they knew the truth.

"I know I just hit you with a lot, but I need to know if you want out of this mission. And I wouldn't fault you for saying yes," Rattler told them earnestly.

Both Spike and Repeat looked at one another and could read each other's minds. Spike smiled and said, "We can't let you have all the fun. Let's get this asshole."

"OK, great—thanks guys. Hopefully in twenty-four hours or so, this will all be behind us and we can start making our way home. I know you both have families… I just wrote my letter home and suggest you do the same. There will be a lot of mission planning, but just treat it like any other mission. We have to let Skipper take the lead so that he doesn't suspect anything, but keep me in the loop if you hear anything weird."

"So, so, so who is flying up front with you if Clipper is flying the other aircraft?" Repeat asked.

"CAG," Rattler replied.

"Oh damn… This *is* serious," Spike replied. "Let's get this done."

CHAPTER 43

Rattler sat in the mass brief and looked around at everyone involved. It was crazy to think that with so many people and all that combined experience, only a handful of people really knew what was going on. As the weather was briefed, Rattler looked over at Skipper. Over the past day, he'd become more sinister-looking. Rattler wasn't sure if this perception was simply a result of his own mental state, but as Rattler watched, Skipper looked over at him and grinned. In that grin was pure evil, and while Rattler merely nodded back, his blood boiled. This man had tried to have him killed and was the reason that Shotgun's kids didn't have a father anymore. It took all of his constraint not to attack the skipper right then and there.

"You OK?" Clipper whispered to Rattler.

Rattler nodded in reply and got his head back into the mission. While listening to the brief and reviewing the mission data cards on his lap, he mentally went over the flight. One of the most valuable traits of a naval aviator is the ability to multitask, a learned behavior from flight school that is honed through countless missions. A pilot needed to be able to review data, listen to a brief, and "chair fly" the mission to ensure that all contingencies were thought of and mentally replayed over and over in readiness for the real thing.

CAG stood up. "Ladies and gentlemen, I am about to send you into harm's way." You will undertake a dangerous mission today, and while my goal is always 100-percent mission success with zero losses on our side, that may not be the case here. We are dealing with an extremely hostile and volatile enemy in the Palestinian Islamic Jihad, and they will stop at nothing to take out both our SEALs on the ground and planes in the sky.

"This is 100-percent real, weapons hot and free, and I expect you to be ready to employ your ordnance with accuracy and precision. There is no room for mistakes, and that's why each of you has been chosen for this mission. As you know, I will be in aircraft 602 with the skipper of the Wallbangers in the back acting as overall mission commander. Communication and command and control will be critical in all aspects of this mission from launch to recovery; therefore Skipper, you will have the hammer on the whole mission. With that, Skipper, the room is yours."

CAG went to sit down as Skipper stood up and moved to the front of the room. Rattler noticed two things: First, CAG was an amazing leader and speaker, but also a hell of an actor. Every ounce of that man wanted to rip Skipper's head off, but instead, he made the skipper feel in charge. The second thing that Rattler noticed was that his skipper had loved every second of it. The junior officers of VAW-117 joked that Skipper had daddy issues or something else from his childhood that caused him to have such a complex, but it was clear that there was some truth behind those jokes. The way Skipper had just walked to the front of the room made one think that he was about to be promoted to a four-star admiral and have an aircraft carrier named after him.

The skipper's display just made Rattler more focused. His anger was gone now that the mission was underway. Launching in a daylight raid against an enemy stronghold with an unknown number and type of weapons was the only thing Rattler cared about. There were already things going wrong with the mission, and Rattler knew that focus was the only way to achieve success. He wanted this to be over and all of this to be behind him.

As Rattler sat in the room, half listening to a man charged not only to lead, but protect, he began counting off the things that had already gone wrong. It was clear that Mr. Murphy from Murphy's Law had already joined this mission and was going to do his best to bring about overall failure. First, this was not supposed to be a daylight mission. Most of the time, the navy operated at night, providing a level of difficulty for the enemy and an advantage to pilots who were comfortable operating at night.

However, intelligence had learned that in addition to everything the skipper had told the PIJ already, they were also working other sides of their game plan to ultimately make themselves more active in terrorist organizations around the world. The PIJ had acquired a small, tactical nuclear weapon that was currently being held at their stronghold in Al Jubail, near the coast in the Persian Gulf. With that weapon in the vicinity, no ship—American or otherwise—was safe in the Gulf. What was not clear was whether they intended to use the weapon against civilian merchant ships or a US warship, or move it from that location to someplace else. At any rate, the Navy SEALs were tasked with taking over the stronghold compound and getting that nuclear weapon before it was used or lost.

Additionally, intelligence given during the mission brief stated that the stronghold was much bigger than previously thought and that the Navy SEALs were going to need more air cover; however, only four Hornets were flagged to go on the mission. While the air wing was working to get more aircraft ready, there were no guarantees. Four Hornets loaded with two AIM 9 missiles, one 500 lb LGB, and one 500 lb JDAM, as well as 500 rounds of 20MM were all that the Navy SEALs would have. While CAG had stacked the deck with his Hornet pilots, that just wasn't much air cover. Skipper had asked for support from the air force, but it was denied, likely due to the sensitive nature of taking down a tyrant in the back of aircraft 602.

Chapter 44

As Rattler opened the hatch leading outside, the sun blinded him. It was a beautiful day, and the unexpected brightness almost stopped him in his tracks. Navy pilots are creatures of habit, and he was so used to opening this hatch to pitch-black conditions on the other side. Not today though. Today it was sunny, which under normal circumstances he would be happy about, but it meant that there was nowhere to hide.

After leaving the mass mission brief, the crews had gone to their individual briefing rooms. The Hornet division talked about where they would position themselves and who would deploy what ordnance in what order. They also discussed what would happen if one or more planes couldn't make it airborne due to a malfunction. There would be no spare aircraft today.

The Prowler crew went to ready room one and briefed their game plan for electronic countermeasures, as well as their tactical and survival protocol, if needed. Rattler and the crews for aircrafts 602 and 604 went to ready room two, initially briefing together and then splitting up to do mission briefs. Rattler was amazed by how quiet CAG was. While he was ultimately in charge of the whole air wing, he knew that the Hawkeye wasn't his area of expertise, and he let the professionals talk as he listened. It was clear to Rattler why and how CAG had risen to his current rank and status.

The only remaining crews for the strike package were the two Super Hornet tanker pilots who went to the forward wardroom to eat after the mission briefs. As a tanker pilot, there wasn't much to brief. They each knew how much fuel they had to give, who to give it to, and where to station. After that, it was time for a burger and some relaxation. In some ways, Rattler envied them.

After the crews from 602 and 604 had briefed together, they split up and briefed as separate crews. It was during this time that Rattler finally spoke as the aircraft commander, going over safety of flight, and for the most part, standard information. He went a little more in-depth than usual due to CAG's presence; he could tell that the Skipper was annoyed by that and had stopped listening. To his credit, CAG hung on Rattler's every word. Perhaps that was because he was a professional, or maybe the lack of ejection seats on the E-2C made him a little uncomfortable. Either way, it didn't matter because Rattler's intent was to bring aircraft 602 and its crew back safely.

After they finished briefing, they went to the PR shop (where safety and survival equipment was issued) and got on their flight gear. Then they checked out their 9-mm handguns from Gunz who was sitting SDO (responsible for ensuring the flight schedule was completed for the day) for this mission, and walked as a crew out of ready room two on their way to the aircraft. Before leaving the ready room, Spool gave high fives to Repeat and Spike, shook CAG's hand, tried to shake Skipper's but was rejected, and then stopped at Rattler.

"Go get 'em, son," Spool said with a firm handshake.

"Yes, sir," Rattler replied as he led the crew to the flight deck.

Usually, the pre-flight check of a Hawkeye is split among the crew, with both the pilot and copilot doing an outside walk around, and the CICO or mission commander pre-flighting the outside of the back and top of the aircraft. Skipper had Spike do that pre-flight because he wanted to get into the plane and make sure the systems were ready to go. It was critical to have two Hawkeyes flying today and Skipper knew it. Since CAG was flying with them, Rattler would be the sole member doing the outside pre-flight while CAG went into the cockpit and was briefed by the PR on how the parachute worked, what to do in an emergency, and how to egress the aircraft.

Rattler worked slowly and methodically outside the aircraft to make sure that everything was perfect. The maintenance personnel might not know exactly what was going on with this mission, but they knew something was up, and they'd made sure that the plane was perfect. Rattler even laughed at how clean it was—almost as if the chief had made his guys clean and wax it too.

After Rattler finished outside, he climbed the stairs to enter the aircraft. He looked back down the tube of the plane and saw Repeat sitting in the first seat. Their eyes met. Repeat looked nervous so Rattler nodded confidently; it was his way of calming his roommate down, and he hoped it worked. As he made his way forward, Rattler continued to check aircraft systems carefully because he didn't have a normal copilot to back him up. Finally, he made his way to the cockpit and sat down. CAG was already sitting in the right seat with his harness connected and was reviewing mission data cards. It was clear that CAG was going to let Rattler do his job and not interfere.

Rattler finished his interior pre-flight checks and continued to review his mission cards until the air boss announced over the 5MC radio to start the aircraft. Aircraft 602 was parked on catapult two and would be the first plane off the flight deck for this mission. Rattler went through his engine start procedure and everything worked as it should. While it was different doing everything himself, Rattler had flown other air wing pilots and VIPs before and handled it just fine. The aircraft had become an extension of his own body, and Rattler was able to get everything up and running with professional precision. Before long, they were unchaining aircraft 602 from the flight deck and maneuvering it onto the catapult for launch.

"I meant to ask, sir, have you ever flown in a Hawkeye from the ship before?" Rattler asked CAG.

"Nope, this is my first time," CAG replied. "So don't fuck it up." He smiled.

Rattler quickly replied. "Yes, sir."

"Ditching hatch removed and stowed," Spike said from the back over the ICS.

"Copy," Rattler replied.

After following the taxi director's instructions, Rattler had positioned aircraft 602 on catapult two, acknowledged the weight setting for the catapult launch based on the aircraft weight, spread the wings, and done his final checks. As the launch got closer, Rattler could feel himself calm down. He was trained to do this and had done it many times before. He was in autopilot mode with his hands and feet going through motions, checking systems, and ensuring all switches were in the correct position without his brain actively thinking about it. At long last, it was time to go. The shooter on the flight deck signaled Rattler to run up the engines. With his right hand, Rattler advanced both throttles to max as the aircraft groaned and the carrier held it in position. Rattler did a full flight-control check and checked all the engine instruments before he was satisfied that the aircraft was good to go.

"Ready, sir?" Rattler asked CAG.

"Show me what you've got, kid," CAG replied.

With that, Rattler saluted with his left hand and then returned it to the yoke. He put his head back against the headrest. His internal clock counted down while on the edge of the flight deck, a nineteen-year-old airman looked forward and back to ensure that everything was clear before pushing the one button in front of him. With that push of a button, the aircraft carrier let go of aircraft 602, sending it from a standstill to flying airspeed within about 100 feet. Rattler was satisfied that everything was operating properly so he raised the landing gear and started the aircraft into a climb onto mission profile. *Let's get this done.*

CHAPTER 45

Even with the severity of the mission and the tension in the air, there was still time to kill. After Rattler got aircraft 602 headed toward the holding position and to the correct altitude, he deselected Skipper, Spike, and Repeat on the ICS. He and CAG would have time to talk. CAG asked questions about the E-2C, and Rattler explained a lot to him. Even with all that CAG had done in his fighter career, the Hawkeye was still foreign to him. While he had flown in one around base to get an idea of what its aircrew were dealing with, he had never flown it at the ship. Rattler figured it had to do with the lack of ejection seats in the Hawkeye. All of CAG's career, he had flown in fighters equipped with ejection seats, and while no one ever wants to use one, it's nice to know that the option exists. Rattler didn't blame CAG for staying away from the Hawkeye.

Spending time explaining the Hawkeye to CAG took the edge off for Rattler, but it didn't change the mission at hand. As Rattler approached the designated holding position for aircraft 602, he quickly switched the TACAN to air-to-air mode to locate Clipper's Hawkeye; he suspected Clipper was right where he needed to be. Things were starting to come together.

"I feel naked up here," CAG said.

"What's that, sir?" Rattler asked.

"Sitting in this plane with no weapons, no defense, and in broad daylight is a weird feeling for me, but I guess you're used to it," CAG answered.

"Actually, I never gave it much thought until I was shot at, and then as dumb as it sounds, I really didn't have time to think about it," Rattler replied.

"Yeah, that was something…shit hot job," CAG said.

"FLIGHT…CICO," Skipper called from the back.

"Go ahead, sir," Rattler replied.

"I need aircraft 604 to move position. Can you relay if I send new waypoints for him?" Skipper asked.

"Yes, sir," Rattler replied.

Skipper sent the new latitude and longitude points for Clipper's Hawkeye, and Rattler quickly plotted them on his map. What he saw made him feel sick to his stomach.

"What is it?" CAG asked.

"He is moving them out of the coverage of the Prowler and closer to the area of operations," Rattler said directly to CAG and not over the ICS in case Skipper was listening in.

"Copy; pass the coordinates. Clipper will know what to do," CAG said out loud.

Rattler got on the radio with Clipper and passed the coordinates. Minutes went by before Clipper radioed back to confirm the points. Once Rattler agreed they were correct, Clipper's voice altered. Knowing Clipper as long as he had, Rattler could pick up on the smallest changes in him. Clipper knew exactly what the skipper was doing, and while it made him angry, he also knew he had a mission to complete. Aircraft 604 moved to the new position and was now flying completely naked with zero radar-jamming coverage or protection from either the Prowler or the Hornet division. Rattler said a quick prayer for Clipper and the rest of 604's crew.

To pass the time, Rattler busied himself with the tasks of a Hawkeye pilot. He ran fuel numbers over and over again and checked on aircraft systems. Maybe what CAG was talking about was right. He seemed to spend most of his flight dealing with the things that were out of his control and trying to stay ahead of them. He couldn't take on more fuel aircraft like the fighters, so he needed to know immediately if the Hawkeye was leaking fuel or had some other malfunction that was causing problems. The sooner he knew the better. He spent the rest of the time listening to any number of different radios and trying to piece together how the mission was going. He knew that all four Hornets had launched, as well as the Prowler. There were two rescue helicopters airborne and another had checked in on alert, ready to launch if needed.

One of the Super Hornet tankers had bad refueling gear and was forced to head back to the ship, but another was about to launch in its place. Both Hawkeyes were operating at 100 percent systems up status, which surprised Rattler. Since pulling out of port after Shotgun died, the overall morale of the maintenance department had been very low. Rattler could see it in the day-to-day stuff around the ship; he was proud of the maintenance guys for banding together and getting these two planes ready for this mission. The fact that CAG was flying with them had most likely played a large part in that extra effort.

Overall, Rattler had a pretty good idea of how the mission was going, and he was sure that Clipper was doing the same mental picture painting in aircraft 604. Trying to maintain overall situational awareness was critical. As soon as the Navy SEALs had intercepted the PIJ and secured the nuclear weapon, they would announce the code word "touchdown" to tell everyone that they had it. Once they were sure that no PIJ members were in control of any surface-to-air weapons, they would announce "going for two" over the radio.

The only people airborne who knew the code words were CAG, Rattler, and Clipper. The plan then was to lock up Rattler's plane with a SAM as if the PIJ had launched a missile. Since Skipper had coordinated with the PIJ to shoot down the other plane, hopefully he would see his scheme going wrong, and confess. It was ironic that the system Skipper had developed to record the mission (an achievement that he was so proud of) was about to be the same system used to convict him of treason. On paper, the plan seemed simple, but it all hinged on the Navy SEALs being on time. Everyone else had to sit back and wait for it all to play out.

"ROLL-EX 30, I repeat ROLL-EX 30," Rattler heard over the radio.

"What the hell?" Rattler exclaimed to CAG.

"FLIGHT–CICO… Everything is sliding thirty minutes to the right. The SEALs are late," Skipper radioed to the cockpit of the Hawkeye.

"SHIT!" CAG said. Aircraft 604 was a sitting duck.

CHAPTER 46

In the cockpit of aircraft 604, Clipper had been doing much the same as Rattler, going over the fuel planning and making sure that all aircraft systems were working properly. He'd known from the start that his aircraft was the bait in this mission, and he was ready for it, but he'd kept that to himself. After having his position moved closer to the area of operation and out of the safety of the radar-jamming Prowler, he'd become hypervigilant. Clipper had heard the same radio call from the SEALs on the ground and knew immediately what that meant. If the PIJ detected his Hawkeye, or were somehow tipped off from the Skipper, then the PIJ would launch immediately, and Clipper would have to spring into action.

If Ratbreath had known Clipper better, he would have realized that Clipper wasn't himself. But Ratbreath was preoccupied with his own thoughts. Although junior to Clipper, he was upset that Clipper was flying in the left seat. He'd wanted to be the one to land on the ship during the day.

"You always get the good deals," Ratbreath said.

"Huh?" Clipper replied.

"The day trap," Ratbreath answered. "I can't tell you the last time I had one of those."

"Well, you are still basically a new guy and relatively speaking, have only been in the squadron for ten minutes, so how about you pay attention outside and keep a good look out. This is a no-shitter mission, and we can't be caught with our pants down," Clipper said. Ratbreath went back to his duties as copilot, pouting like a child. Clipper maintained a vigilant lookout.

"602, 604; you up?" Rattler called on the tactical frequency.

"What's up, buddy?" Clipper replied.

"You copy the new position and Rolex?" Rattler asked, trying to keep the Skipper from getting too curious as to why they were talking.

"Yeah, buddy—I've got it. Copy 100 percent," Clipper replied.

"Copy. Stay safe," Rattler replied.

In the back of aircraft 602, Spike had been going through the normal duties of the air control officer, which included vectoring all of the aircraft to help facilitate tanking and joining up on the Hornets, Super Hornets, and Prowler. All aircraft were now on station and in position, and he had some time to relax. He was uncomfortable because this was the first mission he could remember where he had to stay strapped into his seat for the whole time. After Rattler had told him and Repeat what was really going on, they'd decided that the mission could go sideways at any minute and it would be better to be ready.

Additionally, Spike was trying to keep an eye on what Skipper was doing. With the skipper only about a foot away to his right, Spike tried to go about his tasks as per normal, but it was difficult. He felt like he was cheating on a test while trying to spy on the skipper's scope. One positive was that once Skipper was safely in the back of the Hawkeye, the rest of the world didn't matter; they had him where they wanted him.

Further to Spike's right was Repeat who was going about the normal duties of the radar officer. His job was to maintain the best radar image possible and make sure that all related systems were functioning properly. Since the goal was to try and use Skipper's beloved recording system against him, Repeat recorded all of the internal and external voice communications, as well as data from all three Hawkeye scopes in the back. If this mission came to a successful conclusion, Repeat figured that information might be the needed to help expose the skipper for who he really was.

Spike looked over to Repeat whose eyes were staring at the skipper's scope. Something was wrong and Spike knew it. As he looked over, it was clear what Repeat was concerned about. All three NFO scopes should have looked the same, but Skipper's had a different user interface up that Spike had never seen before. It utilized rudimentary scope symbology unlike the typical Hawkeye instrumentation and featured a top-down view of aircraft 602 and all the aircraft in the strike package around him. When Skipper moved his cursor, it would highlight aircraft type, call sign, and load out. As Spike was trying to figure it out without the skipper noticing, he saw the skipper roll his cursor over the symbol for the Prowler. With a click of the keyboard, a popup came up on Skipper's screen. Spike squinted to read the words, barely able to make them out: "CONFIRM LAUNCH?"

The moment Spike's brain processed what it meant, the skipper clicked "yes."

"Oh shit," Spike mumbled.

CHAPTER 47

"Shocker, missile launch detected, Shocker defending," radioed the Prowler pilot over the strike common frequency.

"What the fuck?" CAG asked.

"Shocker defending east and down; strike package recommends slide 30," the Prowler pilot radioed as he maneuvered the aircraft into a dive to avoid the SAM. The slide 30 call was to tell the strike package that their jamming coverage was now gone as the Prowler was out of the fight, trying to save itself. The Prowler was a four-person aircraft, and while it was a tactical jet aircraft and had countermeasures for such attacks, it was not nearly as maneuverable as one of the Hornets. The Prowler pilot was doing everything he could, but he feared it wouldn't be enough. Within seconds, the pilot was pumping out chaff and flares with his left thumb while trying to visually acquire the SAM. At the last second, he saw the missile rapidly approaching.

"Mayday, mayday, oh shit... Eject, eject!" radioed the pilot. The missile guided and impacted the tail of the Prowler followed immediately by a four-sequence ejection that sent all four crew members in different directions.

"Launch the SAR HELO!" CAG radioed over strike common as the first helicopter began to make its way to the last known location of the Prowler. Another helicopter immediately started its engine on the flight deck, while yet another was being towed into position and readied for launch.

At the controls of aircraft 602, Rattler immediately tensed up: the plan wasn't working. The SEALs had been late, which meant that the SAM launch was the work of the PIJ; moreover, they had been tipped off as to the presence of the various aircraft. Without the Prowler's jamming coverage, all of the aircraft in the strike package were now easy targets. Rattler had to do something, and fast.

"CICO, Flight," Rattler called to Skipper in the back.

"Go!" Skipper replied.

"Sir, recommend mission abort," Rattler stated.

"Negative!" Skipper called.

"Sir, based on your pre-briefed mission criteria, we have lost jamming coverage. That constitutes a mission abort," Rattler pressed as CAG listened in.

"How about you let me be mission commander. You just sit up there, and I'll tell you when I want you to bring me back to the ship!" Skipper shouted over the ICS.

Rattler saw CAG's face turn red. As a single-seat fighter pilot, CAG was not used to flying with NFOs, and while Rattler understood their beneficial role on the aircraft, in this case, the skipper was rogue and needed to be stopped.

"Spike, you up?" Rattler called Spike alone on the ICS.

"Stand by," Spike said.

In the back of 602, Spike couldn't believe what was happening. Still in shock at the skipper's link to the SAM site on the guidance of the Hawkeye radar, not to mention the hit on the Prowler, Spike and Repeat exchanged glances, knowing that they had to do something too. Repeat was working quickly to kill the uplink, or shut down the whole radar if need be. At the same time and to Spike's horror, Skipper was busy working his makeshift system to find aircraft 604. Almost in slow motion, while Repeat worked feverishly to cut the communication, Spike saw Skipper select the other Hawkeye with his cursor. He clicked, prompting the same on-screen question: "CONFIRM LAUNCH?"

"Sir, what screen is that?" Spike asked to distract the Skipper and buy Repeat some time.

"Mind your own business!" Skipper replied.

"Sir, I can't let you do that," Spike said as he lunged for the skipper, but it was too late. The fate of 604 was sealed.

"Missile in the air…604, move!" Spike radioed over strike common.

The radio call echoed through every cockpit in the strike group. Sitting in aircraft 604, Clipper's world immediately stopped. He had no idea where the missile was and how long it had been airborne. Ratbreath froze in fear; Clipper sprang into action.

"Hang on!" Clipper said over the ICS. He disconnected the autopilot on the Hawkeye and pushed the nose over to gain airspeed. He knew roughly where the missile might be coming from, and his eyes methodically scanned the sky. He actually wanted to head toward the area, hoping that he would gain sight of the missile and be able to defeat it.

Things all started to happen at the same time now and very quickly. While Clipper was desperately trying to defeat a missile he had yet to see, Spike and Repeat in the back of the other Hawkeye were trying to understand what the skipper had done. Repeat was finally successful in getting the radar offline without the skipper knowing. On the aircraft carrier, XO Spool was in the classified command center and had been in communication with all of the aircraft, as well as the Navy SEAL commander on the ground. Satisfied that there were no friendly forces in the area, he made the call.

"99 Hail Mary, I repeat Hail Mary," Spool said over strike frequency. With that call, each pilot in the four F/A-18s reached up and selected their master arm switch to "arm," launching a total of four JDAM smart bombs destined for the PIJ training camp. Those PIJ members were done.

In the back of 602, Repeat had terminated the link between the SAM site and both Hawkeyes' radars. Clipper had just visually acquired the SAM and was beginning to work on defeating it when he saw it trail off behind his aircraft and eventually fall out of sight.

"99 the SAM is down, 604 is safe," Clipper said over strike common.

"Is everyone OK?" Clipper asked his crew. He received affirmative answers from the NFOs in the back. But when he looked over at Ratbreath who was staring straight ahead, Clipper realized that his copilot was anything but OK.

"How are you doing, man?" Clipper asked. Without a word, Ratbreath vomited all over himself.

"Well, I guess that answers that," Clipper joked.

"99 touchdown; I repeat, touchdown," radioed the lead Hornet pilot of strike common. All four bombs had made their impact, and it looked like the Navy SEALs would be busy doing a battle damage assessment instead of a takedown. Rattler sat in the front of 602 and finally breathed a sigh of relief.

"All aircraft return to mother," XO said over strike common, and in the perfect unison that was naval aviation, each pilot went about their normal duties to get their aircraft back to the ship.

"CICO, Flight," Rattler called to the back.

"Go ahead," Skipper said.

"Sir, they are recalling us to the ship. Are you ready to go home?" Rattler wondered what was going on in the back of his plane and how much Skipper understood.

"Looks like we don't have a choice," Skipper said.

Rattler couldn't get a read on the skipper or what was happening. He seemed calm and almost dejected that his mission didn't go as planned. Rattler was going through the motions of getting the plane back to the aircraft when he heard Spike call him.

"Dude, can you hear me?" Spike almost whispered over the ICS.

"Yeah, dude—what's up?" Rattler replied, being sure to select only Spike so that no one else could hear them.

"It's all recorded… We got him, bro," Spike said.

A huge grin swept across Rattler's face, one so big that CAG couldn't help but notice. All of the pain and loss of life that his skipper had caused would not be in vain. That recording meant that this skipper's career was over.

"Something you need to tell me, son?" CAG asked.

Rattler pulled his boom mic down to be able to talk out loud and not over the ICS. "They recorded the whole thing in the back, sir. We have all the evidence we need to hang him," Rattler yelled over the noise of the cockpit.

"Take us home, son," CAG replied with a smile as he leaned back in the seat.

CHAPTER 48

Rattler went about normal procedures and checklists to bring the plane down from altitude; he did his best to not be distracted by the success of the secret mission. With the information that Spike and Repeat were able to record, there was no way that Skipper wouldn't be linked to the PIJ. Rattler figured that he would ultimately be tried for treason. There was some empathy for the skipper's wife and kids (who likely had no idea how deranged he had become), but he felt worse for Shotgun's family.

Rattler monitored both the strike common and tactical frequencies on his way back to the ship. It was clear that all four Hornets had successfully executed bomb strikes on key targets, and the Navy SEALs were in the process of cleaning up the leftovers. Once back at the ship, he would hear the full debrief on the targets they hit, and they would ultimately learn how much intelligence the skipper had sold to the enemy.

Rattler was also happy to hear that the Prowler crew was successfully recovered. All were unharmed except for the pilot who had a broken leg. They were onboard two helicopters and heading back to the ship and would likely be there shortly after Rattler landed. He was extremely happy that no more loss of life had occurred during the skipper's take down. Lastly, Rattler had talked to Clipper on tactical radio to make sure that he and his crew were OK. Clipper reported that other than Ratbreath puking on the right side of the cockpit, everyone was fine. But just to be safe, Clipper was going to do a straight-in approach to the ship.

For the first time in a while, Rattler finally felt at ease. His life had seemed to be spiraling out of control since the divorce, but now he felt a sense of calm. He had learned the truth about his skipper and answered the call when asked to help take him down. The only thing he needed to do now was land on the ship without incident. The skipper would be escorted by the military police and likely put in the brig until they figured out where to transfer him. Perhaps the skipper would stay in the brig for the whole trip back home... The idea of him eating bread and water for a month while being locked up on the ship didn't bother Rattler one bit.

"Do you have the COD in sight?" CAG asked.

"Got them, sir. I will plan the break to come in right over them," Rattler replied. "So, sir—have you ever heard of a Hawkeye shit hot break?"

"I thought it was a myth. Remember, it's hard to impress a fighter pilot," CAG said with a grin.

"Yes, sir." Rattler smiled as he pushed up the throttles and dropped the nose of the Hawkeye to gain airspeed.

Rattler controlled the Hawkeye like it was an extension of his own body. As CAG looked on, Rattler timed it perfectly to show up right behind the ship at 800 feet just as the COD was about to land. Prior to even crossing over the ship, he rolled the Hawkeye into a sharp angle of bank to the left, pulled hard, and reduced the throttles to idle. In one fluid circle behind the ship, Rattler bled off airspeed and configured the plane for landing. He completed the landing checklist and when he rolled wings level, the landing area was clear. He was three-quarters of a mile behind the ship and on glide slope. Rattler worked hard to keep the plane in the perfect place all the way down until the wheels slammed into the flight deck and the arresting hook caught the three wire, bringing the big Hawkeye from flying speed to a full stop in seconds.

After the aircraft had stopped and was clear of the wire, he went about folding the wings and taxiing the plane to be parked on catapult number two. He'd been the last plane to land, and the only thing on the flight deck was the COD parked in front of the tower with the engines running while they off-loaded their cargo. Rattler went about shutting down the Hawkeye, and CAG got out of the seat to keep Skipper in his sight. The prebriefed plan was to keep the MPs out of sight until Skipper got off the plane. Then he would be handcuffed and brought to the brig. Rattler finished shutting down things in the cockpit and was the last to leave aircraft 602. He patted the door, thanking the aircraft for keeping him safe.

The flight deck was noisy with the COD engines running, but Rattler could see CAG and Skipper having an animated conversation near the tail of the Hawkeye. CAG got right in Skipper's face. He said something else to him and then reached onto the skipper's flight suit and ripped off his name tag with his wings on it. He then walked away, signaling for the MPs who were waiting out of sight.

Time slowed again as Rattler watched the scene. CAG was walking away, and the skipper was reaching for his gun, finally realizing that his career, and likely his life, were both over; he had nothing to lose. As the skipper unholstered the 9-mm gun from his survival vest and went about taking aim on CAG, Rattler took off running. Instinct kicked in and Rattler was a kid again, back on the football field. Coming from behind the skipper, he knew he had the advantage, and he either wanted to tackle him or knock him so far off balance that he would drop the gun.

A sense of rage filled Rattler as he sprinted full speed toward the skipper. He was closing ground quickly, and just as Skipper brought the gun up to put the sights on CAG's back, the MPs saw what was happening and they trained their guns on the skipper. CAG noticed this and turned around in time to watch Rattler hit Skipper square in the back, knocking him off balance. One shot rang out from Skipper's gun straight up in the air as the skipper stumbled forward from the force of the hit. CAG watched the look on Skipper's face as he finally realized he couldn't stop his forward motion. The skipper closed his eyes a split second before the COD's turning propeller impacted his body, shredding it immediately. Death was instantaneous.

The COD pilots shut down the motors, but it was too late. There would be no incarceration, no bread and water, and no trial for the skipper; his fate had been decided on the flight deck of the aircraft carrier. As the engines of the COD came to a stop, Rattler sat on the flight deck, surveying the scene, completely exhausted. The flight deck of the USS *Nimitz* had fallen unusually silent.

Epilogue

ONE MONTH LATER

"How about another beer?" Sandy asked.

"That sounds great," Rattler replied.

It had been a month since the mission ended and things had started to calm down. Data from the Hawkeye had been given over to the intelligence community and more had been found in the skipper's stateroom. He had been selling secrets to the PIJ for a long time and had an offshore bank account filled with money to prove it. The air wing and aircraft carrier set sail for home in the days following the mission, and Rattler and his squadron mates did their best to return to normal routines.

XO Spool had been promoted to Skipper, and his first act was to sit the officers of the squadron down and explain everything to them. Some were shocked and others less so. Rattler sat at the back of the meeting room, quietly processing everything that had happened. As usual, news aboard the ship spread quickly; Rattler became known for taking down a skipper who, in everyone's mind, got exactly what was coming to him.

Rattler spent most of his remaining time on the ship thinking about what his next set of orders would be and trying to figure out how he would spend time with Sandy. He had been through a lot, and she'd been there for him more than his ex-wife ever had. He wasn't sure where the relationship was going, but he wanted to enjoy the ride with Sandy for as long as he could.

A few hours ago, as the carrier approached the dock in San Diego, Rattler and Clipper stood on the flight deck, looking into the crowd. Sandy had agreed to meet the ship, and in the distant sea of happy people waiting to meet their loved ones, Clipper picked out Sandy and pointed her out to Rattler. Rattler felt bad for his friend who hadn't heard from Cheri since the port call in Perth. In fact, no one had heard from her since.

Rattler spent the rest of the afternoon showing Sandy around the aircraft carrier before finally leaving and heading to a hotel in Coronado. They showered and got ready to meet some squadron mates to celebrate the homecoming at the local bars. The energy and vibe were all positive as members of the air wing and ship looked forward to some time off. Rattler had finally relaxed and was enjoying every minute of it.

"The next round is on me," CAG said, approaching the two from behind and holding three beers.

"Thanks, sir." Rattler took one and gave one to Sandy.

"I've got something here with your name on it." CAG pulled out an envelope from his pocket. It was addressed to LT Jack Owen, USN.

"Sir, what is it?" Rattler asked, taking the letter.

"Orders," CAG replied.

"To where, sir?" Rattler asked as he opened the letter.

"VFA-106, NAS Oceana, Virginia. You've been selected for a transition to fly the Hornet, son. Congratulations," CAG said, holding out his hand to Rattler.

"Thank you, sir." Rattler was in shock, and Sandy hugged him around the waist. Rattler shook CAG's hand, trying to believe that his lifelong dream of being a fighter pilot was coming true. Considering everything that he had been through, this was almost too much to handle, but he did his best to be in the moment.

"Son, I know we haven't really talked about what happened on that flight deck, but you will never buy a drink in my presence again, understood?" CAG said.

"Yes, sir," Rattler said, standing up a little taller.

"To Rattler!" CAG yelled, raising his glass.

"TO RATTLER!" everyone yelled.

As everyone in the bar cheered, Sandy turned Rattler around and came in very close so that he could hear.

"Does this mean that I'm dating a fighter pilot now?" Sandy asked with a wink.

"It sure as hell does," Rattler replied. He pulled her close and kissed her.

www.ingramcontent.com/pod-product-compliance
Lightning Source LLC
Chambersburg PA
CBHW030811310726
48980CB00006B/462/J

* 9 7 8 0 5 7 8 8 9 8 0 7 0 *